SO FAR APART

So Far Apart

by

Louise Armstrong

Dales Large Print Books
Long Preston, North Yorkshire,
BD23 4ND, England.

British Library Cataloguing in Publication Data.

Armstrong, Louise
    So far apart.

    A catalogue record of this book is
    available from the British Library

    ISBN 978-1-84262-727-3 pbk

First published in Great Britain in 2008 by
D. C. Thomson & Co. Ltd.

Published in Large Print 2010 by arrangement with
Louise Armstrong

Dales Large Print is an imprint of Library Magna Books Ltd.

Printed and bound in Great Britain by
T.J. (International) Ltd., Cornwall, PL28 8RW

Chapter One

Trespassing!

An owl hooted. Kayleigh Hartley gulped nervously, but kept moving forward. Cold chills ran down her spine.

'Did you hear that spooky bird?' her startled companion cried.

'Shh!' hissed Kayleigh. 'Keep your voice down, Tom.'

But it was too late. A dog barked loudly. Lights flashed on, illuminating the big house and the lawn. French windows flew open, and a large male figure rushed out on to the terrace.

'Stop or I'll shoot!' he commanded.

Kayleigh's legs shook. The man was holding a long-barrelled shotgun. She'd been caught. Panicky thoughts galloped through her mind. What if she ended up in court? Her mother would be so upset. Though a court case would bring a lot of publicity for the campaign, she supposed, and that might help the badgers, but was it worth it?

'Let's get out of here!' Tom urged.

Kayleigh gripped his arm. 'Don't run! Don't do anything to provoke him.'

'Wise advice, if a little late,' the gunman sneered. 'You have already provoked me by wandering around my lawn in the middle of the night.'

A hefty female form ran out of the house and thundered towards them, swathes of taffeta skirt billowing around her.

'Hugo? Hugo? Is it burglars? Shall I ring the police?'

'Yes,' shouted Hugo.

She was followed by another male figure, carrying a powerful torch.

'Wait a moment!' he commanded. This man sounded calm and amused.

'Hugo's caught some burglars, Daniel! How exciting!' the female squealed.

The bright torch flashed in Kayleigh's eyes, then ran over her body, lingering on the large plastic black and white badger that she had gripped in her hand.

'These people appear to be delivering something rather than absconding with your property,' the calm male voice observed.

Kayleigh could only see a large dark form behind the light. The amusement in his voice grated. She reached up to brush blonde hair

8

out of her eyes and realised that her hair had escaped from its plait.

'So, do I ring the police or not?' the female shrieked.

'We don't need the police,' the calm male voice advised.

'Of course we do,' Hugo snapped. 'They're clearly up to no good.'

'Wait, Hugo. It looks like a student prank to me. You don't want to look foolish.'

'These people are trespassing on my property.' Annoyance grated in Hugo's voice. 'How does that make me the fool in this situation?'

Nevertheless, he suddenly turned to the woman. 'Put your phone away, Fiona.'

He gestured at Kayleigh and Tom with the barrel of his shotgun. 'Come up on the terrace, you two.'

Feeling all kinds of a fool herself, Kayleigh walked towards the long paved terrace that ran the whole length of the house as Hugo snapped on an outside light.

He, Daniel and the woman perched on the stone wall that bordered the terrace, while Tom and Kayleigh stood facing them.

'Oh, man! This is heavy,' Tom muttered.

Kayleigh examined the three people before her. The woman, Fiona, was tall and chunky. Her ball gown was the wrong shade of pink for her freckles and reddish hair, and there were far too many frills on it. Hugo was wearing a dinner jacket. He, too, was large, running to fat, and he had porky jowls that bulged over his white fine-knit roll-neck sweater. The other man, Daniel, was lean, dark and handsome, and Kayleigh had to admit that he looked very good in his evening clothes, but his blue eyes were regarding her with a mixture of disdain and tolerant amusement that scraped her nerves raw.

Fiona's brown eyes suddenly went wide. 'I say! Why on earth are they carrying those revolting plastic animals around with them?'

Daniel's smile grew wider. 'Can you see a fluorescent label around the neck of each animal? I think you'll find an explanation written there.'

Hugo gestured to Daniel with his gun. 'Get one and read it.'

Daniel raised a dark eyebrow. 'Shouldn't you put that gun away, Hugo?'

Hugo scowled, but he did snap open the long barrel of his gun, and as two orange cartridges fell out into his hand, Daniel's expression was astounded.

'I can't believe you're carrying a loaded

gun! What are you thinking? This is Cheshire, not the Wild West.'

'A man has a right to protect himself,' huffed Hugo.

Daniel's laugh was deep, rich and easy. 'I don't think these scruffy urchins are much of a threat.'

Once Hugo had set the gun aside, Daniel went indoors and came back with a red coat that he wrapped around Fiona.

'You mustn't get cold,' he commented solicitously.

To her astonishment, Kayleigh was smarting inside. She often dressed down because she didn't like people judging her by her blonde prettiness, but she certainly didn't like being written off as an urchin by a stuck-up man in a tuxedo! And she'd had enough of standing around in the cold.

She turned to the lad beside her. 'Come on, Tom, let's go,' she said, and turned on her heel.

'Wait!' shrilled Fiona. 'I want to know what's going on.'

Hugo scowled horribly. 'I demand that you come back.'

Tom hesitated, but Kayleigh grabbed his arm. 'Come on – he won't shoot us,' she encouraged.

'Come back!' Hugo thundered, but Kayleigh kept on walking, towing Tom behind her.

'Excuse me.' It was Daniel's voice, calling after her. 'Would you be so kind as to explain the meaning of your plastic badgers to us all?'

She stopped. Wasn't this whole exercise about spreading the message? So she turned back.

'You know the new bypass?'

'It's wonderful,' Fiona gushed. 'Town is positively civilised now.'

Hugo's dark brows snapped together over his brown eyes.

'Got it! You two are part of that gang of troublemakers camping in the lay-by on the new road. I've seen your mess and slogans everywhere. Scruffy disorganised lot. I should call the police after all. And don't give me any of that "saving the world" hogwash. You lot like causing trouble, that's all it is. You're not bright enough to understand the politics of town planning. You're simply against progress because it *is* progress, and because you're too lazy to get a proper job. You'd rather live on benefits and pretend you're morally superior to those of us who do a proper job and work hard...'

'Hugo,' Daniel said, with a bite in his voice that made Hugo stop and listen. 'Let the young lady explain.'

Hugo's brown eyes glinted with annoyance, but at least he subsided.

Kayleigh took a deep breath.

'The trouble with the new road is that it goes right across an ancient badger path. Badgers don't understand roads. They try to cross at the same place they've always used, and they get squashed.'

Hugo looked down his nose at her. 'So?'

'So, we want the council to build an underpass for the badgers.'

Fiona gave a great squeaky squeal of laughter. 'You cannot be serious! Do you know how much that would cost?'

Kayleigh did, actually. She had a copy of the blueprints and an engineer's estimate sitting in the bedroom at home.

'We're raising money towards it,' she said. 'That's where the plastic badgers come in.'

She held out her badger and everybody looked at the large black and white beast. Hugo stepped forward and snatched at the bright label tied around the animal's neck. 'The Build a Badger Tunnel Campaign', he read. 'Phone the number below. For a donation of one pound (or more) we will

13

come and remove this animal from your premises. For a donation of five pounds (or more) we will re-home this badger on a lawn of your choice'.

Hugo's eyes narrowed. 'What made you target me?' he demanded.

A certain person had donated a hefty sum to their campaign in exchange for teasing Hugo, but Kayleigh decided it would be wiser to keep that secret.

'You have a nice lawn,' she replied, suppressing a smile.

Hugo glared, and his shoulders flexed menacingly, but Daniel put a restraining hand on his arm. 'Leave it, Hugo. They're harmless enough.'

Fiona gave her squeaky laugh. 'They're useless pests.'

Kayleigh shook her head. 'We want to save the badgers.'

'We've got a cool website if you want to know more,' Tom piped up.

Fiona laughed again. 'Gosh, no!'

'I want to know who sent you here,' Hugo growled.

'It's a random campaign, Hugo,' Daniel said peaceably, 'and not to be taken seriously. The local justice of the peace found three of the little critters on his lawn last week. He found it very amusing, and I happen to know that he made a substantial donation to have them relocated to his mother-in-law's garden.'

He turned his cool gaze on Kayleigh and Tom. 'I suggest you two take your badgers and vanish.'

'Fiona, it's time I took you home.'

This time Kayleigh let Tom tug her away.

The outside lights went off and peace returned to the dark night. Big clouds swept across the dusky sky. There was no need to hide now, so they walked down the long sweep of the drive that ran from the front of the house through the lovely green of the grounds to the road.

'He was one heavy dude,' Tom moaned.

Kayleigh sighed. 'I don't think we made many converts tonight.'

'We never even left a badger. Do we have to give back the donation?'

Kayleigh thought for a minute.

'No. We made our point, and no-one can see the garden from the road, so the donor must have known that only Hugo would see the badgers.'

Tom walked along in silence until they reached the bushes where they had hidden their bicycles. He was evidently brooding on his encounter with Hugo.

'Complete sense of humour failure,' he said, shaking his head.

'Total,' Kayleigh agreed.

She waved to Tom as he set off towards the antique purple camper-van that was his home at the eco-camp, then turned in the other direction to cycle back to her penthouse flat in the city.

The roads towards Manchester were never empty, but the traffic was light and she enjoyed the exercise. The tyres hummed and the trees rustled over her head and the miles vanished as she pedalled, thinking over the events of the evening.

She was more shaken than she had admitted to Tom. Without the intervention of the man called Daniel, the encounter could have been very unpleasant, even dangerous. She thought Hugo was a man with a frightening amount of anger in his personality. There must be a reason for it, she reminded herself, but still, it had been terrifying to stare down the barrel of a loaded gun. Thank goodness for Daniel.

She ought to be grateful for his calm control, yet his air of detachment had irritated her. He'd known about their campaign, but he didn't seem to care about the badgers. She wondered if he cared about anything deeply, and if he'd been Fiona's date. Surely not! She wouldn't be right for him at all.

She wondered what they had all been doing before she had interrupted them. They looked as if they had been to a very glamorous party. Oh, well, it was nothing to do with her.

Kayleigh spun into her elegant cul-de-sac, cued the remote control that opened the garage door, and popped her bike into the rack next to her car. She would miss this lovely big garage when she moved next week.

As she walked up the stairs to her apartment, she found herself remembering Daniel's handsome face. What a shame that she'd met him in such inauspicious circumstances. She chuckled. Part of her psyche considered his dismissive reaction a challenge. It was a real shame she was unlikely to meet him in full make-up and a posh frock, because she would like to see his face when he realised how wrong he'd been to write her off as a grubby urchin.

Chapter Two

Familiar Faces!

By the time morning came Kayleigh had recovered from the fright of the night before and whistled cheerfully as she ran down to open the garage and get out her car. You couldn't win them all, and now it was Monday morning and time to concentrate on work and her new client.

The weather was fine and springlike so she put down the top of her little two-seater and enjoyed the sunshine as she sped across town to the factory she'd been asked to visit. The directions to Bond's Cycles were easy to follow, and, despite the traffic, in under an hour she was pulling into the parking lot of a factory on the outskirts of Manchester.

A tall man with steel-grey hair, hazel eyes and a calm face was waiting for her in reception.

'Miss Hartley? I'm Peter Warner-Bond,' he said. His expression barely changed as he greeted her, but she knew he was having the usual reaction.

What was it that made people think that a young and pretty blonde couldn't have a good mind? But Kayleigh had an excellent qualification in Marketing and Business Studies and an excellent salary to match.

Once they were settled in his office with cups of tea, he surveyed her with a smile.

'You're very young to have achieved so much! I do hope you can help me. I have a problem that has me quite at a loss.'

Kayleigh relaxed. 'That's my trade,' she assured him with a smile.

Peter smiled back. 'I should tell you right from the outset that I seem to be alone in my concern; the rest of the board think I'm overreacting, but I must admit that I'm worried.'

'Can you start by telling me a little about the business?'

'All our bicycles are hand built. They always have been, since the business was started by my great-grandfather. When the motor car took over, it seemed for a while as if we might have to close, but children still buy bikes and, of course, mountain biking became popular. A few years ago, we started making a premium sports range, and they have taken off in a most unexpected manner. In fact we need to expand in order to keep up with demand.'

Kayleigh nodded encouragingly. 'Go on.'

Peter stirred uneasily, then reached for a large folder and pulled out a plan of the factory and surrounds. It showed a medium-size cluster of buildings with a large area of land running down to the ring road.

'You used the small car park at the front of the building, didn't you? You can't see the back of the factory from there. You might want to take a look at it before you go. We thought it would be ideal for our new buildings, but there were a good number of trees growing there.'

'Ah!' Kayleigh said, suddenly understanding a great deal. 'And you need the land at the front of the factory for your car park, I suppose.'

'Indeed. I'm afraid most of our employees drive to work.'

'Please don't say you cut all the trees down.'

Peter looked uncomfortable. 'We had a survey done first, which showed that their roots were damaging the walls of the factory, and the borough council granted permission.'

Kayleigh looked crestfallen. 'Oh, dear!'

'We have been considering expansion on to that land for a good number of years, and it has been zoned for industrial use for over one hundred years. Great-grandfather would never have bought the site without it.'

'But you make mountain bikes! Your customers will care about environmental issues.'

'I'm afraid nobody considered that. Planning permission for the expansion was granted on Monday, but I gather it would never have been allowed if the trees were still standing. It doesn't look good. I have had an email from a – an eco-warrior, do you call them? – accusing me of underhand practices.'

Kayleigh nodded. 'You're right to think there may be serious consequences.'

The expression in Peter's hazel eyes was worried. 'I'm afraid I've been very stupid,' he said mournfully.

'You're not stupid at all. What about your architect, your builder and your factory manager? Don't you pay all those people to advise you?'

Peter looked no happier. 'They think I'm being alarmist. And I am satisfied that we have acted legally, and in good faith, but still, there is no denying that the situation is not ideal. It does look rather unfortunate.'

'Well, it's no good crying over fallen trees,' Kayleigh said, thinking rapidly. 'Don't worry, Peter. You're quite right to take this seriously, but I'm sure the situation is recoverable, especially if you act quickly. Let me think ... there are several angles to consider.'

He gave her a relieved and delighted smile. 'Would you be prepared to talk to the board?'

'Of course.'

'Excellent! I'll get everyone together...'

The boardroom was oak-panelled and old-fashioned. Two people in dark suits were already sitting at the table when Peter escorted Kayleigh in. Peter introduced them as the sales manager and the finance director. Silence fell, then the door crashed open and two women hurried in. Peter sprang to his feet.

'Ah, Ruth, my dear, may I introduce you to Miss Hartley? Kayleigh, this is my wife, Ruth Warner-Bond.'

Ruth was tall and thin with dead straight grey hair. There was no warmth in her brown eyes, but she spoke politely. 'Hello, Miss Hartley. How nice for Peter that you were able to come.'

However, it was the other woman Kayleigh couldn't drag her eyes from – a large woman with ginger hair who wore a red coat that clashed horribly with her colouring. 'And this is Fiona Morton…' Peter was saying.

It was the woman from last night! Kayleigh felt as if she had a stone in her stomach. What a situation to be in!

She waited for Fiona to scream and order her out of the room, but the woman was looking at the factory plans that had been unrolled on the boardroom table.

'Peter, have you been telling Miss Hartley about Hugo's marvellous factory expansion? He masterminded the entire operation, you know.'

The name 'Hugo' sent a cold chill through Kayleigh, and then the man himself marched into the room. He looked at Kayleigh and the anger in his malevolent brown eyes made her wince. She waited for him to throw her out, and wondered how she would explain losing the job to her new boss. But even as she tensed her shoulders, Hugo turned to Peter.

'Are you seriously considering wasting money on a rubbishy public relations company?'

'Miss Hartley comes highly recommended

and she thinks, as I do, that some kind of action is needed to compensate for the trees that were destroyed.'

Kayleigh took several deep, calming breaths as the two men continued to argue. It seemed incredible that neither Fiona nor Hugo had recognised her. But it *had* been dark last night, and she probably looked very different in a business suit with her blonde hair pulled back in a neat chignon, but still, could they be so unobservant?

As if things couldn't get any worse, at that moment Ruth jumped to her feet. 'Here's Daniel.'

Ruth's brown eyes lit up as he strolled into the room, while Kayleigh wasn't surprised to see the trio that she had met the night before completed.

Peter introduced Daniel as his son.

'I'm glad you could make it, Daniel,' he added. 'I was afraid that your work would prevent you from attending, as usual.' His last words were acid.

'The hospital is understaffed as always,' Daniel said calmly. 'You know it's some-times impossible for me to attend meetings.'

Peter's hazel eyes were intense. 'The family business should come first.'

Daniel's calm expression didn't change as

he said, 'I'll never give up medicine,' but there was a sharp undercurrent to his voice.

'We need you here, Daniel,' his father said urgently.

Hugo's fist thumped the table. 'What for? I don't need any help to run this company.'

Ruth coughed loudly.

'May I suggest that we deal with the pro-testors as the first item on the agenda?' Her words were polite, but her tone suggested that she expected to be obeyed.

Kayleigh saw Peter glance at his wife and visibly recall the situation.

'That's a capital suggestion. Daniel, I'm glad you're here today. If everybody would care to take a seat?'

A secretary came in to take the minutes, and Kayleigh sat at the polished table, glad of a few minutes to collect herself while Peter went through the formalities of open-ing the meeting.

She was used to sizing up the atmosphere when she met with a new client. She guessed that the confrontation between father and son was a long-running battle, and it was one that she had met before. In her view it was a mistake to force an unwilling family member into a business, and at least it did look as if Daniel had got his own way in taking up another career, but clearly his father still wanted him to be more involved in the business.

Next she examined Hugo, glowering in his place at the end of the table. He seemed to be responsible for the day-to-day running of the factory, and Kayleigh's questions about his exact relationship to the business were answered when Peter said, 'Bert Morton sends his apologies, as usual. Copies of the power of attorney held by his children, Hugo and Fiona, are on the record and they will, of course, be able to vote in his stead.'

Kayleigh relaxed slightly. Now she understood the business set-up. The one outstanding question was Daniel. Had he recognised her or not?

She examined the man thoughtfully. Whereas Hugo fumed and fidgeted through the necessary formalities, Daniel sat quietly – too quietly, perhaps. He wasn't relaxed but held under a tight control. There was tension in his jawline and in the set of his shoulders. He seemed wary, and somehow aloof from the other people at the table.

As if he felt her observation, he looked up and met Kayleigh's gaze. His clear blue eyes sparkled like a precious stone, the pupils very black and velvety. For a long moment he was unsmiling, and then his eyes lit with a warmth and charm that she couldn't help responding to, and she smiled back. Even if he had recognised her, he wouldn't give her away.

Peter had reached the first item on the agenda: tree felling. He said, 'I think we should respond to the complaint that has been made.'

Fiona's face screwed up in anger. 'But that's insane! We've done nothing wrong. Hugo says that an injunction will take care of him if he becomes a pest.'

'Who has contacted you?' Kayleigh asked.

'He goes by the name of Mole Man,' Peter told her. 'He has emailed me, and tried to get into the factory yesterday. Hugo advised me not to meet with him, but I confess that I feel uneasy about the whole matter.'

Ruth looked cold and displeased. 'Peter, I can't understand why you're taking that grubby youth seriously. Hugo said that the lad was positively feral. The police will take care of him.'

'It's a mistake to judge anyone by appearances,' Kayleigh interjected with feeling, but Ruth was not to be deflected.

'Hugo is more than capable of dealing with one scruffy protester. I'm surprised you doubt his judgement,' she told her husband, but Peter stood his ground.

'The young man has a point. Without understanding the sequence of events, it does look as though we removed the trees in a somewhat underhand manner.'

'What rubbish!' Fiona butted in furiously. 'Hugo went to enormous trouble to make sure all the permits were legal. That filthy youth is nothing but a yob and a trouble-maker.'

Kayleigh looked at Peter. 'You said you haven't spoken with him?'

'No, he sent an email which my secretary printed out for me to read.'

Kayleigh had come to a decision. A whole campaign formed in her mind, if she could only get them to agree to the first step.

'Peter, you need to meet with this young man and listen to what he has to say–'

'Society has gone completely mad and so have you,' Fiona screeched in horror. 'How can you possibly suggest that we even con-sider dignifying such a pest with a response?'

'Peter needs to meet with him to find out what he wants,' Kayleigh pointed out firmly, and saw Peter nod, but Ruth looked doubtful.

'I wish everyone would stop acting as if

Peter has committed a crime. All he has done is expand his own factory on his own land,' she said.

The finance director spoke for the first time. 'I can't understand why we're discussing this at all, or why Peter has brought in a stranger. Leave it to Hugo. It's his job.'

'It's not that simple…' Kayleigh began, but again Fiona interrupted.

'Miss Hartley, it's wicked of you to cause all this trouble. Do stop stirring things up.'

'I say we vote on it,' Hugo put in. 'Let's not waste any more time.'

Peter cleared his throat. 'Yes, let's do that. I vote we hire Miss Hartley to handle what could be a public relations disaster.'

'No!' Hugo bellowed.

'No!' Fiona and Ruth chimed at the same time.

The finance director and the sales manager both voted no, too.

Kayleigh turned to look at Daniel. In a way his vote didn't matter, since the majority was already against her, yet she found herself holding her breath. She looked into his clear eyes and wished she could read his mind.

He looked at her for a long moment before shaking his head and saying, 'No.'

That was that then. Kayleigh stood up to

leave, and smiled at Peter.

'Feel free to call me if you'd like to talk anything over.'

Ruth gave her a cool, dismissive nod. 'Thank you for your time, Miss Hartley.'

Hugo snorted and turned away. Fiona glared at her with vicious dislike in her brown eyes.

In defiance of the general disapproval, Peter stood up and kissed her warmly on the cheek.

'Thank you for coming. I would prefer to follow your advice, but I must bow to the wishes of the board.'

Kayleigh let out a huge breath as the door of the boardroom swung closed behind her. She'd been to some tense meetings, but never one where she'd been in fear of being unmasked as an eco-warrior and expelled from the room!

Her mobile rang as soon as she switched it on. It was her new boss, Nick Corkish.

'Did you get the business?' he demanded.

'No,' Kayleigh admitted.

'Then bill them for a day's consultancy.'

'What? Joan never charged if we weren't hired.'

'Joan has retired and sold the business to me.'

Yes, and now you're changing everything, thought Kayleigh. But he was the boss.

'OK. I'll follow your rules in future, but this referral came from Joan, and she'll have told them that the initial consultation is free.'

She could almost hear Nick thinking.

'From now on we do it my way,' he barked.

'Sure,' Kayleigh agreed, grinning. It was as close as he could come to admitting that it would be wrong to charge the bicycle company.

'I'm going to the plastics manufacturer now, if that's OK. He wants to discuss a campaign to promote his conservatories.'

'OK, but be back by four o'clock. We've got a new customer coming in and she asked for you.'

Kayleigh jumped into her little roadster and set off for the next call of the day. She was good at what she did and she enjoyed it. In a few moments, she would turn her mind forward to the rest of the day, but first she spent a few minutes mulling over the last encounter.

Meeting those three people again had been so bizarre, one of those odd tricks fate sometimes played. As for their situation, she thought Peter was right and it needed careful handling, and she could have done a lot for them. But maybe it was as well they hadn't hired her. She wouldn't have wanted to be in the way of Hugo's reaction if he suddenly realised who she was!

She would love to know if Daniel had recognised her, but he was so cool and controlled there was no way to tell what he was thinking, though she had a feeling that he hadn't been as oblivious as the other two. She grinned to herself. If she ever met him again, she would ask him, but it was very unlikely.

Chapter Three

In The Early Hours...

Two nights later Kayleigh sat bolt upright in her bed, her heart thudding loudly in her ears. It wasn't a dream, her telephone was ringing. That was what had wakened her. She tried to stay calm, but a premonition sprang into her mind.

'It's probably one of the eco-warriors,' she tried to tell herself, grabbing for her dressing-gown with shaking hands and tripping over her slippers in her panic. 'They'll need bailing out or something, that's all it will be.'

She snapped on the light, blinking in the sudden brightness, and picked up the receiver anxiously. 'Hello?'

'Kayleigh, love, it's Mum. Now, you're not to worry...'

Kayleigh went cold all over. 'Mum, you sound upset. What's wrong?'

'Your sister's had an accident. She was out with John on that motorbike of his. I'm at the hospital now. Oh, Kayleigh...'

Kayleigh held tight to the receiver and tried to marshal her thoughts. Her lips were shaking so that the words would hardly come.

'Mum, don't cry. I'm coming now. Is Dad with you?'

'Yes, he's here, and so are your brothers. I'm all right. You don't have to come. Go back to bed.'

'As if I could!' Kayleigh muttered as she hastily donned some clothes.

She barely kept to the speed limits as she hurried across a chilly and deserted Manchester to the hospital. Cars and ambulances were arriving and leaving, but Kayleigh was able to park her little convertible right in front of the building in the kind of space she imagined you would only find at 4.30 in the morning.

The hospital was very warm inside. There was a young man on duty at a reception desk and she hurried towards him.

'My sister...' She struggled to control her whirling mind and make sense. 'She was in a motorbike accident. Her name's Charlene Hartley. Where will I find her?'

The man smoothed down his hair, leaned over the counter and winked.

'I'll find out for you and then take you

there myself. How about that?'

Kayleigh felt anger jump into her throat. Was he … flirting with her? At a time like this?

'I'll manage. Just tell me where to find her, please.'

At her tone, the receptionist puffed out his cheeks and looked sulky.

'I was only being nice.'

Slowly he ran a broken pencil down the list of names on the screen of his computer. As she waited, Kayleigh caught a glimpse of herself in the mirror behind the desk and sighed. Life would never let her forget her extreme good looks. In some ways it was nice, of course, but pretty blondes weren't allowed to be serious, brainy or upset. She was sick of having her feelings brushed aside while people reacted to her looks.

She rapped on the desk. 'Hurry up, will you, or do I have to ask your supervisor where my sister is?'

He gave her a mean look, but finally muttered sulkily, 'Intensive Care – this building on the top floor.'

Kayleigh went up six floors in the lift and then walked down a long corridor, listening to her footsteps echo, dreading what she would find at the other end.

Her whole family was gathered in a small waiting-room. Her chubby father sat next to her mother, patting her knee gently, his normally jolly face solemn, and Kayleigh suddenly realised how grey his hair was turning. His eyes lit up when he saw her and he nudged his wife, who sprang to her feet, tears welling in violet eyes that were the same shape and colour as Kayleigh's. Kayleigh hugged her hard, finding comfort in the familiar smell of her flowery perfume.

Before anyone could speak, the door opened again and a police officer walked in followed by a dumpy middle-aged woman who Kayleigh recognised as the mother of Charlene's boyfriend, John.

'How's Charlene?' the woman asked, tears in her voice.

'We don't know, love,' Bill Hartley said. 'The doctors are working on her. They told us to wait here. How's your boy?'

'John's fine – just a broken arm. They're keeping him overnight to be sure, but he's fine. It's Charlene he's worried about.'

Kayleigh's skinny teenage brother Kevin was eyeing the policeman.

'Are John and Charlene in trouble?' he asked.

'No, son,' the officer replied. 'Not as far as

I'm aware. We have to wait for the full report, of course, but young John's breath test was clear, his bike was roadworthy and it seems he was riding well within the speed limit. He was unlucky, that's all – swerved to avoid a joy-rider, apparently.'

Kayleigh's older brother, Bailey, usually resembled his good-tempered father, but now his face was distorted with worry and anger.

'Have you caught them?' he demanded.

'Not as far as I'm aware, sir.'

Bailey clenched his big builder's hands.

'Thieves and criminals! Not a scratch on them and my sister may be dying! What are you doing standing around here? Get out there and catch them!'

Bailey's wife, Sandra, gently touched his arm. 'I'm sure they're doing all they can, Bailey. Take it easy, love.'

His 19-month-old son, Tommy, toddled over and hugged his father's leg. 'Daddy cross!' he announced.

Bailey's blue eyes softened and he picked up his son and kissed him.

'Yeah. Sorry, mate. Sorry, everyone.'

Sandra relaxed and smiled at her husband with her beautiful dark eyes, while Tommy chuckled and kissed his daddy back. The police officer didn't exactly smile, but he did say calmly, 'That's all right, sir. I can understand you're worried.'

'You can say that again!' Bailey said fervently.

The policeman took a few details from Kayleigh's mum, and once he'd left, her dad went to see the ward sister yet again, but he came back shaking his head.

'She just keeps saying Charlene's still being operated on and they're doing all they can.'

Sandra got to her feet and pushed back her cloud of dark hair.

'I'll have to take Tommy home and feed him. In all the rush I never thought to bring a bottle. I'll come back when we're done.'

There was still no news when she came back an hour later. Tommy was too young to know what was happening, so he played happily on the floor with his red truck, then, after an hour or so, he settled down for a nap. Kayleigh sat on a hard plastic chair and waited.

'I'm glad John's not in trouble with the police,' Mrs Hartley said.

Kayleigh sighed. 'Even so, I can't help blaming him. Everyone knows how dangerous motorbikes can be.'

As tears slipped down Mavis Hartley's cheeks, Mr Hartley put his arm around her.

'More coffee, anyone?' he asked.

'I'll have a cup, Bill.' Sandra sighed. 'Anything's better than looking at those dreary health posters. How's the house move going, Kayleigh?'

'The sale is signed and sealed,' Kayleigh answered, 'and I move out on Tuesday.' She didn't feel like chatting.

Mr Hartley suddenly looked at his watch and said, 'Goodness, it's nine-thirty! What about work, Kay? Have you told them where you are?'

'I'll tell them later.'

'Tell them now. You're one of the bosses now, don't forget – you have to set a good example.'

Knowing her dad was right, Kayleigh took the lift down to the ground floor and went outside, where a refreshing breeze ruffled her hair and cooled her hot dry skin. There was a tiny grassy garden next to the car park, and she stood there to use her mobile to call her secretary.

'Hello, Rona? It's me.'

'Kayleigh! Where are you? I guessed something was wrong so cancelled your first appointment. I hope that was all right.'

'Thank you. Actually, I won't be in at all today…' She explained about her sister's accident.

Her secretary briefly expressed sympathy, then quickly returned to the topic of work.

'The fund-raising campaign for the wild-life sanctuary can wait, but what about the hotel photographs? Have they been approved? The brochure needs to go to the printers today and be back by the end of the month.'

'The photographs are fine. I've signed them off and put them in the safe. But, Rona, please treat my charity work with the same importance as you do my other clients. Don't make them wait.'

'Sorry, Kayleigh, but Nick said not to bother with it.'

Nick again.

'I see. Then I'll discuss it with him later. Thanks for everything, Rona. I appreciate your support. Now I must get back – I might be missing news about my sister.'

Kayleigh ran back into the hospital and charged up to the waiting-room, but nothing had changed, and the family sat on the hard plastic chairs for another two and a half slow, creeping hours.

At midday, a tall doctor in a white coat

finally walked into the room. Kayleigh should have been astonished to see it was Daniel, but she was too worried about Charlene to wonder about the way fate kept throwing this man at her. Her parents rose and stared at him fearfully.

'We've done all we can,' he said, looking around the room briefly. 'All we can do now is wait.'

'Will she be all right? Will her leg be all right?' Mrs Hartley asked.

'Barring complications, she should make a reasonably recovery.'

'Complications? What do you mean?' she pressed fearfully.

Daniel's eyes were tired and his expression was distant. Kayleigh was sure she saw him smother a yawn.

'There is a potential risk with any surgery, although the procedure went as well as can be expected.'

'As well as can be expected! Will she walk again? I must know.' Mavis clutched at his sleeve. 'You're the doctor. You did the operation. Surely you can tell me if she'll walk again.'

Tension vibrated strongly in the room. Kayleigh almost heard Daniel's temper snap.

'Being a doctor does not make me a clairvoyant.'

There was a moment's appalled silence. Mrs Hartley turned away, tears sliding down her crumpled face, and she looked achingly old and vulnerable. Kayleigh's own temper rose in her like fire.

'How dare you speak to my mother like that?'

Daniel's eyes were still blazing. 'Do you not realise how much worse today could have been for you all?'

He spun on his heel, slammed open the door and left the room, but Kayleigh was determined to have her say and raced after him, chasing him down a long polished corridor, dimly aware that her older brother was running after her, but not letting that stop her.

'You have no right to speak to my mother like that! She's worried sick about Charlene.'

Daniel stopped by a closed office door, his hand on the doorknob. His eyes were blazing.

'Your sister has had the very best of medical care and attention and with any luck she will make a good recovery. Be thankful for that! Do you want me to enumerate the terrible complications that could have occurred? She is alive and doing well. What else matters?'

A small part of Kayleigh knew he was right, but she was too furious for common sense. She felt Bailey's strong hands catch her from behind, gripping her arms so that she couldn't spring forward, but he couldn't stop her from shouting, 'You pompous stuck-up toad!'

Daniel's nostrils flared, and he lifted his chin in a haughty manner as he opened his office door.

'I'm afraid this area is restricted to medical personnel, so we will have to conclude our little exchange.'

As the door banged in her face, Kayleigh yelled, 'You come back here! Who do you think you are?'

'Leave it, Kay.' Bailey was still holding her tight.

'I won't forget this,' she promised. 'I'll come back tomorrow and hunt out that snooty snob and give him a piece of my mind.'

When they got back to the waiting-room, her mother and father weren't there – they had been allowed in to the intensive care ward to see Charlene.

Ten minutes later they came back, smiling

45

with relief.

'She bandaged up like Frankenstein's mummy, but she's awake, and she knows us. She's chatting like nothing was wrong.'

Kayleigh went in next with Bailey. Their little sister was lying in a high-tech bed surrounded by machines that hummed and hissed; tubes criss-crossed the coverlet, and a pump sighed regularly behind her. She looked at them with bright awareness.

'You'd better have a look at this amazing ward while you can, because they're chucking me out in ten minutes.'

The nurse standing next to the bed smiled. 'Charlene doesn't need to be here any more. She's come round from the anaesthetic perfectly.'

Knowing that Sandra and Kevin were waiting to spend a few minutes with Charlene, Kayleigh kissed her then returned to the waiting-room, where a sweet-faced nurse was talking to her parents. The nurse looked up at Kayleigh.

'I've explained a bit more about the operation to your mother,' she said, and despite herself, Kayleigh was soothed by the nurse's manner. 'We can't give guarantees, but Mr Warner-Bond is one of the best surgeons in the world. You're so lucky that he was in the hospital when Charlene was brought in, and even though he'd already been operating for eight hours, he stayed for another seven to rebuild your sister's leg. He could have gone home, but he didn't.'

Seven hours! Kayleigh felt her anger evaporating. Then she remembered what had triggered the scene.

'He was very rude to my mother!'

'I did pester him, love,' Mrs Hartley conceded.

'That's not like him at all,' the sweet nurse added gently. 'He's usually charming. He must have been exhausted.'

'Seven hours on his feet,' Kayleigh said thoughtfully. And given how demanding the work of a surgeon must be... 'That's long enough to wear anyone out.'

'An *extra* seven hours,' the nurse reminded her. 'He's been operating for fifteen hours without a break.'

Kayleigh's hands flew to her mouth.

'I didn't realise how shattered he was.' Remorse crept into her heart as she reinterpreted the scene. 'I thought he was pompous. I was awful to him.'

The nurse smiled at Kayleigh with kind eyes.

'His voice is a bit posh, but he's a lovely

man. We all love working with him. I expect he was dead on his feet and you misread his manner.'

Kayleigh felt hot and guilty as she realised how badly she'd misjudged the man. He'd had every right to yawn!

'Will you tell him I'm sorry?' she said in a very small voice.

'Poor man,' said Mrs Hartley thoughtfully. 'After all he did for our Charlene. I'll have to make him a cake.'

Kayleigh felt wonderfully comforted. Charlene was awake and talking, and her mother was thinking about baking a cake. The worst of the crisis was over!

Chapter Four

Forgive and Forget?

Contrary to the warning Daniel had felt obliged to make, Charlene recovered rapidly from the surgery. She was only on the high-dependency ward for twenty-four hours, and after two days in an ordinary ward, the hospital loaned her a wheelchair and let her come home.

'Almost a full house,' said Mrs Hartley on Sunday, beaming around her crowded living-room with satisfaction in her kind eyes. 'I do like having you all home.'

Kayleigh rustled among the papers from the estate agent.

'I won't be staying with you for long, Mum,' she promised. 'I can't wait to find the next house to do up. I'm going to visit some properties today. There're lots to look at.'

'I can see that!' her mother said. 'I never knew there were so many houses for sale in Manchester, and I've got pictures of all of them spread over my living-room carpet!'

Charlene's blue eyes lit up. 'House shopping! Can I go with you?'

'Don't let her!' Kevin shouted from his position lounging on the sofa hogging the TV remote control. 'Who wants an old peg-leg hobbling around their house?'

'Don't wind her up, Kevin,' Mavis said. 'You can't go out this weekend, Charlene, love. I want you resting at home. And don't mess with your plaster cast.'

'I have to scratch under it – I'm itching!' Charlene complained.

When the doorbell ding-donged, Charlene's hazel eyes brightened and she sat up expectantly.

'You go, Kevin. Jadine said she'd call round!'

'Like we want more of your ditsy school-friends visiting,' Kevin grumbled, but he went to answer the door.

Mavis went back to the kitchen, and Kayleigh carried on sorting through house details. The hardest part of even spare-time property developing was finding the next one to do up. She appraised a picture of a large Victorian house. It would turn into nice flats, she decided, but wondered if she was being a bit too ambitious for what was, despite the advantages of having a builder for a brother, only a hobby!

A powerful scent of roses and fresh greenery made her look up. To her utter astonishment, Daniel was standing in the doorway, clutching a huge bouquet of flowers.

Kayleigh felt overwhelmed by surprise and embarrassment, and an uncomfortable feeling she had no trouble identifying as guilt. This man had freely given his time, dedication and skill to repair her sister's leg, and she had flown at him like a fishwife.

'Dr Warner-Bond!' Charlene cried. 'Cool. You found us! My boyfriend didn't believe I was getting a home visit!'

'This is exactly a home visit,' he said, smiling, 'although I might have to admire my handiwork while I'm here. You know I've come to see your mother.'

As Mavis arrived in the lounge doorway all of a fluster, Daniel's lovely blue eyes were grave and sincere.

'I want to apologise for my appalling behaviour on Thursday. I had no right to lose my temper with you. I am so sorry. Will you forgive me?'

His apology was so complete, his smile so charming, the overall appeal of the man so devastating, that Kayleigh could understand

51

why her mother needed no more persuasion to capitulate.

'I'm not surprised you snapped, love. Your nice nurse told me how long you'd been working that day, even before you started on our Charlene. Wrong, it is. They wouldn't let a lorry driver work those hours. It wouldn't be legal. I know that, because our Bill worked as a driver, you know, before he retired.'

'Is Mr Hartley in? I could perhaps have a word with him.'

Mavis's hazel eyes crinkled in a fond smile. 'On a lovely day like this? He's up at the canal, fishing. He loves his fishing, does Bill.'

Daniel proffered the flowers. 'Will you accept them with my most sincere apologies?'

Mavis looked at him with astonishment in her eyes. 'For me? Well, I never saw such a bunch in all my days! What's this in the middle then?'

'I think it's bamboo,' Daniel replied gravely, but with a nice smile in his eyes. 'And these are orchids. I think that's a lily, and I feel pretty safe in saying that the pink ones are roses.'

'I'll have to see if I've got a vase big enough,' said Mavis, taking the bunch from him. 'And as it happens, I'm just icing a cake for you. You'll have to come into the kitchen to see it.'

Daniel's face was a picture. 'A cake?'

'You're not the only person who feels bad about what happened, you know. I was all upset at the time, it's my only excuse, but I never said a word of thanks that night for all you did for our Charlene. It's true what you said to me: when I think of the tragedies some folk have to stand, I should have been grateful instead of pestering you.'

'That's very generous of you,' Daniel said.

'Come in the kitchen – see what I've got for you.'

As she ushered him out, Kayleigh stayed in the lounge, feeling awful. She wished she could join them. She wished she could walk into the kitchen and say that she was sorry, too, and could they be friends, too, but it was as if some kind of invisible glue kept her stuck to the carpet, staring unseeingly at a leaflet bearing the details of a completely un- suitable brand-new family house in North Manchester.

By the time her mother and Daniel came back they were the best of buddies, with Mrs Hartley calling him Daniel and him calling her Mavis. He had come in clutching a massive bunch of flowers, and he would be leaving clutching an equally massive white cake box, but for now he put it on the floor by the door and went to see his patient.

'Your mother is very talented,' he told Charlene as he examined her toes with gentle fingers. 'The nurses are going to go mad when they see this cake! I'm on duty this afternoon, so I'll take it straight to the hospital, although it's a shame to cut into such a work of art.'

'It needs eating, love,' Mrs Hartley told him. 'It's a sponge cake underneath, so it won't keep like fruit cake does. Get it eaten today.'

Kayleigh watched Daniel's kind face and gentle, competent hands as he examined Charlene and then smiled at her with warmth in his eyes.

'I know you won't believe me just yet, Charlene, but your leg is doing very nicely indeed. I'm pleased with it.'

'Will I have a limp?'

'There is that possibility,' he conceded. 'You did extensive damage, I'm afraid. We'll have to wait to see how it heals. Try not to worry until then.'

Charlene bit her lip. She was keen on sport and had even talked about becoming a

PE teacher. Kayleigh felt sorry for her, but she knew her little sister was lucky to be alive. She was glad to see Charlene making an effort to smile and speak casually.

'It itches,' she complained with a giggle.

'Good, that means it's healing. When's your next appointment?'

'Next week. Thursday, isn't it, Mum?'

'That's right, love – the twenty-fourth. But it's not with you, Daniel.'

Kayleigh couldn't believe how thoroughly she had misjudged this man. There was so much kindness in his smile as he looked at Charlene and her mother.

'That's because you don't *need* to see me again. The doctors at the clinic will take care of you from now on.'

He turned away and picked up his cake box ready to leave, and Mavis went to the front door with him. Kayleigh wanted to go, too, but she couldn't break free and get up off the carpet. She just couldn't move.

She heard the front door of the house open, and then shut. He was leaving and she hadn't spoken a word to him.

She strained her ears and heard the sound of a car engine starting outside. This was her last chance.

Suddenly her paralysis lifted and she jumped up. Her feet felt clumsy but she rushed out of the room and through the front door into the sunshine. Her mother was standing on the path, waving. Daniel was in his car at the kerb, leaning forward, nodding and smiling through the window, about to drive off.

Kayleigh raced down the path and put her hand on the passenger door.

'Wait!'

For a second his eyes met hers through the glass, and then he turned off the engine and got out, narrowing his eyes against the brilliant sunlight. He didn't say anything to make starting the conversation easier. He just stood looking at her, and then shifted position slightly, so the sun didn't dazzle him.

She heard the front door click behind her as her mother went into the house, and smiled. 'Mum's very tactful, but you can guarantee that Kevin will be peering out of the window.'

'And what might he hope to witness?'

Kayleigh took a deep breath in.

'Me, apologising properly for losing my temper. I'm sorry for the way I yelled at you. So very sorry.'

Her words seemed to break some tension,

and he smiled ruefully at her. 'I deserved it.'

Kayleigh breathed out. 'Can you forgive and forget?'

He laughed. 'I'll forgive you easily enough, but I wish it was that easy to forget. My new nickname in the hospital is *Mr Toad!*'

For a moment Kayleigh didn't understand, and then her hand flew to her mouth.

'Oh! I didn't think anyone was around.'

'There is always someone around in a hospital, especially when one of the doctors is being told that he's a pompous toad. Never mind, I expect they'll get tired of making croaking sounds in a week or two.'

She couldn't help laughing a little at his woeful expression.

'I am sorry, truly.'

His eyes smiled into hers and her knees went weak.

'A little teasing won't hurt me. And it's making work more fun for my team at the moment. I've never heard them laugh so much. It's a pity they're laughing at me, of course, but I do like my staff to be happy.'

'I don't know how serious you're being,' Kayleigh said, feeling a little breathless.

A lawnmower roared into life and the breeze brought the scent of grass as Mr Harper across the road got going on his garden.

'Smells like spring,' Daniel commented, breathing deeply. 'I should get out in the open air more often.'

Kayleigh was glad that he seemed in no hurry to be off. His big luxurious car sat idle at the kerb, paint and chrome winking in the sunlight. He followed the direction of her gaze.

'I don't suppose you approve,' he said. 'It's not very eco-friendly.'

Her gaze flew to his face. 'So you *did* recognise me!'

His eyes were very bright and intense and she felt shy as she met his gaze, her heart beating fast. She wished she could think of something light and casual to say, but he spoke first.

'You know, you puzzle me. When I first met you I thought you were a complete drop-out, then I saw a polished and controlled businesswoman in action, and next I'm attacked by a complete virago.'

'And now?'

He was looking at her, examining her face with a mixture of surprise and pleasure in his eyes.

'And now I find a warm and charming family woman. I'm glad you came out after me. I did owe your mother an apology, but truthfully I was hoping to speak with you.'

'Me?'

'Would you consider coming out with me one evening?'

'I'm not doing anything tomorrow,' she said eagerly, and could have bitten her tongue off. She looked at the ground in mortification. 'The Rules' had just gone out of the window, that was for sure. Its authors said that men preferred women who played hard to get.

She looked up at his face, and was relieved to see his broad smile.

'Thanks. Believe me, I'm not playing any games with you when I say that my only free night for some time to come is Friday next week. I'm just a doctor with a full list and several business trips coming up.'

'Next Friday is fine,' she said.

Daniel got an electronic organiser out of his pocket but as soon as he checked his diary he looked exasperated.

'Oh, I forgot – I've promised to meet my parents at the opera next Friday. We've taken a box, so there'll be a spare seat. Would you mind joining us? We can have dinner alone afterwards.'

'The opera?' Kayleigh said doubtfully. 'I don't know anything about opera, except that I don't think I like it.'

'Ah. Are you free during the day?'

'Not really.'

'Not even for lunch?'

She thought of her office with its ever-busy computer screens and the phones that rang incessantly.

'We used to have a flexi-time arrange-ment, but now I'm only allowed half an hour. I usually eat lunch at my desk.'

'That's bad for your digestion,' Daniel said absently. 'Then we're looking at the first Saturday in June. Are you free?'

'Well, yes, but … can't you ever go out during the week?'

He shook his head. 'I'm very boring, I'm afraid. I have a personal rule of early nights when I'm working, no coffee, and certainly no alcohol.'

Kayleigh put her hand on his arm, wishing she could find the words to express her emotional turmoil.

'You're so dedicated. I can't believe I was so rude to you. I'm truly sorry.'

He looked at her in such a way that she realised he found her attractive, and for once she blessed her pretty face, because she wanted him to like her.

He made no effort to move closer or to

touch her. Only the light in his blue eyes betrayed the warmth of his feelings as he said kindly, 'You were worried about your sister. That's very natural.'

Kayleigh thought quickly. If he could deny himself coffee, surely she could tackle opera? She wanted to see him, she really did.

'I'll come to the opera with you, then. I'd love to.'

He grinned, the pleasure clear in his eyes. 'Good. It would have been a shame to have to wait until June for our first date. The opera's at The Lowry in Salford. I could pick you up around six, so we would have time for a drink with my parents first, if that was convenient for you.'

'Lovely,' Kayleigh said, privately wondering what she had let herself in for. 'What's the show?'

Daniel quirked an eyebrow. 'The opera is called *Madame Butterfly,* by an Italian called Puccini.'

'I'll look forward to it.'

She stood in the warm sunlight and watched his tall body climb gracefully into the car, then admired the competent way he drove his gas-guzzler down their busy street. Then she turned to walk into the house, clutching her stomach and thinking, *Madame Butterfly!* Well, there are enough butterflies in my stomach right now!

When she walked into the kitchen, her mother was sitting at the table fashioning yellow roses out of icing sugar.

'I'm going to the opera with Daniel, Mum,' Kayleigh told her.

'Opera? Well, that'll be another first for you.'

'I'm a bit worried about it, though.'

'Why? You might like it. You loved skiing once you got up those mountains, remember.'

'I know, but what if everyone is posh and I feel out of place?'

Her mother gave her a swift smile. 'Anyone can do anything these days if they put their minds to it. And the world's a better place for it, if you ask me. You stick up your chin and tell yourself you're as good as the next person, if not better. Look how far you've come already.'

'Thanks, Mum,' Kayleigh said, reaching out a hand to steal a petal of icing.

Her mother tapped her hand. 'Stop that! I'll save you a rose if you go and tidy up those house leaflets of yours.'

'OK,' Kayleigh said, leaving the kitchen.

But instead of continuing her hunt for a suitable investment property, she went upstairs to inspect the contents of her wardrobe, and then urgently rang her best friend, Tracy, to ask her what a girl should wear to go to the opera.

Chapter Five

First Kiss...

Kayleigh was almost ready when Daniel arrived on Friday evening; she heard him go into the lounge and start talking to Charlene. A few minutes later she ran downstairs, and when she pushed open the door, his expression was openly admiring.

'Get you, Kay!' Charlene said. 'Give us a twirl!'

Kayleigh obliged, spinning so that her skirts flew out.

'Is it posh enough?' she asked Daniel. 'I thought I'd have to wear a long dress and lots of jewellery but the girl in the shop said that people don't dress formally for the opera these days.'

He looked at her ballet-length black dress and the pretty Chinese brocade jacket that went over it.

'Your outfit is exactly right,' he reassured her. 'Your shop girl knew her stuff. You would have been overdressed in an evening gown, although I'm sure you would have looked fabulous!'

Kayleigh smiled at him. He was wearing a smart but ordinary dark suit with crisp white shirt. Then she noticed that his green silk tie was decorated with a pattern of cartoon toads.

Seeing she had noticed, he smiled. 'It was a gift from my team at the hospital.'

'Oh no! Are they still teasing you?'

He grinned cheerfully. 'Yes, and it's entirely your fault. I'll have to extract a forfeit later.'

She felt a delicious thrill run down her spine as she wondered about that forfeit. A kiss, perhaps?

Mrs Hartley stuck her head into the lounge. 'Be off with you or you'll be late!'

Kayleigh kissed her mother and Charlene, and waved to Kevin, watching from the window.

As she got into the car she looked at Daniel's handsome profile and couldn't help wondering what it would be like to kiss him. He gave her a quick glance before he set the car in motion.

'OK?'

'All buckled up,' she answered, snapping home her seat belt. Then she sank back into the plush leather seat. 'I shouldn't like this car, but I do!'

'I'm fond of it myself, though I suppose you think I should cycle everywhere?'

'Not everywhere. I have to run a car myself. But I do cycle if I can.' Kayleigh chuckled. 'Besides saving money, the traffic is so bad these days it can be faster.'

Daniel gave her a swift glance. 'Who are you this evening? Am I in for a lecture on saving the world?' There was a definite sharp note in his voice and Kayleigh felt chilled.

'I'm being myself, saying what I think.'

'Wanting me to change.'

'I didn't say that. I said that I cycle sometimes.'

She looked out of the window. Was the evening going horribly wrong? But then Daniel said. 'You're right. I'm sorry. Defending myself from disparagement is becoming a way of life with me – I see criticism where it doesn't exist.'

Kayleigh turned to stare at him, astonished. 'Who could criticise you? Your nurse told me you're one of the best surgeons in the world.'

'I wish she would tell my father that,' he returned ruefully.

Kayleigh was fascinated by the depth of

feeling that simple comment revealed, but Daniel firmly switched the topic to neutral matters and kept them there until they arrived at the theatre complex in Salford.

The sky was light with the sharp distinct colours of sunset and big pink and orange clouds floated over the modern buildings. It was cold in the multi-storey car park and Daniel insisted that Kayleigh wrap his over-coat around her shoulders. It felt strange, but very nice, to be snuggled up in fine cashmere that smelt of lemon cologne and to be tenderly escorted towards the glass and steel entrance of the Lowry Theatre.

'Have you been here before?' he asked.

Kayleigh shook her head. 'I'm not very arty, I'm afraid.'

Daniel's eyes sparkled.

'Why apologise? You're perfect just as you are.'

As she walked into the theatre lobby, Kayleigh hoped that his parents would share his opinion.

She quickly looked around at what every-body was wearing, but there wasn't a long frock in sight. Most of the women looked like Daniel's mother, who was wearing a plain, though very stylish, black sweater and skirt. Her only concession to dressing up was a silk scarf the colour of spiced rum to match her eyes, and long amber earrings. Daniel kissed the air above Ruth's cheeks and then shook hands with Peter, smart in a roll-necked sweater and blazer. Their greeting seemed very cold to Kayleigh.

'Been having any more trouble with eco-warriors, Dad?' Daniel asked.

'Thankfully, no,' his father said. 'It looks as if we can start the expansion. But I do wish you would take an interest in it.'

'You need a trained project manager, not a tired doctor,' Daniel replied reasonably.

Peter shrugged. 'Perhaps you're right. Hugo will take care of it.'

'But he doesn't know anything about building work, does he?' Daniel said. 'It might be better to get in a specialist.'

His mother shook her head at him. 'You've never been fair to Hugo, darling.'

Daniel's mouth tightened. 'Being your godson doesn't make Hugo an expert at everything!'

'Let's not have that conversation again,' Peter intervened. 'Clare Woolford sends her regards. Did you know they've sold their farm?'

Kayleigh noticed that Daniel and his parents stood about two feet away from one another as they chatted. It was odd how distant they were, and how disapproving. Most parents would be bursting with pride to have a son like Daniel, but she could sense a definite tension.

The theatre bar was modern, with large areas of glass. Through the huge windows Kayleigh could see that the sky was a deep navy blue now, and hundreds of lights glimmered on the water of the Salford Quays. She was about to draw Daniel's attention to the beauty of the scene, but a sturdy woman in orange, red and pink rushed up to them.

'Hello, Peter. Hello, Ruth. Daniel, how lovely to see you!' she gushed.

As the Warner-Bonds greeted Fiona, her companion, a greyhound-thin man, drifted to a stop beside Kayleigh. Fiona completely ignored him.

'Hello,' Kayleigh said, feeling a bit sorry for him, but he didn't say a word in reply. He had a very shy face, she noticed.

Daniel turned, a smile in his eyes as he drew the two women together.

'Kayleigh, you've met Fiona, haven't you?'

Fiona's mud-coloured eyes flicked dismissively over Kayleigh.

'Oh, yes. Weren't you trying to sell us something a few days ago? One gets so many salespeople pestering one…'

'Kayleigh works in public relations, Fiona. I'll get you a white wine. Another drink, Kayleigh?'

'Yes, please.'

As Daniel walked off to the bar, Fiona turned to Kayleigh. 'Are you one of those people who hand out leaflets? I think street flyers ought to be banned. Nobody reads them, and they make such a frightful litter.'

Kayleigh tried to keep her reply neutral. 'You're right, so our agency tries to hand out items that people will keep. You can fit quite a lot of information on a packet of tissues, for example, and market research tells us that most people will be pleased with a free pen.'

Fiona shuddered theatrically. 'I hate market researchers! They *will* try to stop one when one is in a rush. I spent at least ten minutes trying to shake this ghastly woman yesterday. I kept telling her my car was on a meter, but she wouldn't stop asking me questions about toilet cleaners. It wasn't until I said that if I got a parking ticket I'd send it to her company that she finally let me go. I couldn't believe how dense she was, but I suppose one has to develop a thick skin in your line of work.'

Kayleigh felt chilled by the malice in Fiona's muddy-coloured eyes and looked around hopefully for Daniel, but he was still at the bar. The shy man kept his eyes on Fiona and said nothing, and Kayleigh was feeling very alone, so she was pleased when a deep voice remarked, 'I'm sure most people would enjoy an opportunity to stop and talk with Kayleigh.'

His intervention worked, for Fiona turned away to say to Daniel's mother, 'Isn't the traffic terrible, Ruth? It took me at least fifteen minutes to get into the car park.'

Kayleigh spoke softly to Peter. 'Thank you! As you know, I don't actually do that kind of work any more, but I did start at the bottom, and that did mean handing out leaflets.'

'You specialise in damage control now, don't you?'

'Yes. I enjoy it, and it's important. One bad story in the Press can cost someone their career, or ruin a company.'

'I wish more people understood that,' he remarked gravely. 'I think we've been very lucky at Bond's to have the tree-felling incident fade away.'

Kayleigh was glad when Daniel came back with the drinks, then stood close by her side, a reassuring warm presence. The talk turned to music, and suddenly Fiona's companion came to life. However, Kayleigh didn't understand a word he was saying so she found it a relief when a bell went to tell the audience to take their seats in the theatre.

'I'm afraid we won't see you in the interval, darling,' Daniel's mother said to him as they entered the box. 'We've promised to have a drink with the Byrons.'

'Shall we meet for a quick coffee afterwards?' Daniel asked.

'Lovely,' she replied, as the lights went down.

Kayleigh tried to listen to the music, but it was just a noise to her. She read the subtitles displayed on screens at the side of the stage, concentrating hard to see if following the story helped, but the plot seemed unrealistic and silly and she looked around in despair. The actual theatre was lovely, big, modern and comfortable, but the stage sets and the costumes were bare and ugly-looking. Since when had Japanese people dressed in newspapers and old sacking? There was nothing pretty to look at.

She sat suffering the noise and struggling to follow the plot, but it was a relief when it all crashed to a halt and the lights went up.

The evening was turning out to be a case of enduring each moment, she decided, while Daniel's parents went off to meet their friends and he went in search of ice-cream. As soon as he came back, he asked the question she was dreading.

'So, what do you think of it?'

She waved her ice-cream spoon. 'Gorgeous. Lemon and ginger is my all-time favourite flavour.'

He raised his eyebrows and gave her a look that said, 'No nonsense!'

'I was expecting kimonos and Japanese gardens,' she confessed, and he laughed.

'I must admit, I'm with you on that one. The look of this production is most unappealing. I much prefer a traditional setting. But it's the music that matters – would you agree with that?'

She could have been cowardly and agreed, but she decided she might as well be honest. 'I can't make head nor tail of it,' she admitted. 'The singing's too screechy for me to follow, and I can't work out the plot at all.'

Daniel took her hand in his, threading warm, comforting fingers through hers.

'You don't need to follow the plot. In fact,

opera makes no sense at all if you think about it. You *feel* it, in your heart. That's the way to experience the music. Open yourself to the emotion.'

It was strange advice from someone who seemed so buttoned up, Kayleigh reflected as the lights went down, yet she found it very easy to follow. She stopped reading the subtitles and worrying about what was happening on stage and just let the music flow into her heart, and it was like suddenly getting a clear signal on a radio. The music poured over her in a glorious flood. She was enraptured by the whole of the last act, and she was still crying when the lights went up.

'I never knew opera was so beautiful,' she whispered.

Fiona came barging into their box like a red and orange firework, her companion trailing silently behind her.

'Come on!' she bellowed. 'I'm starving. Let's beat the crowd out of the car park.'

'Kayleigh and I will follow you in a minute,' Daniel said.

Fiona looked at Kayleigh's tear-stained face then turned to Daniel's mother.

'I thought the performance was rather lame tonight, don't you agree, Ruth? The orchestra was positively barbaric.'

But Daniel's mother's brown eyes were soft and thoughtful as she looked at Kayleigh.

'Perhaps one can be too critical. I think they played with real feeling.'

Kayleigh blew her nose and turned to Daniel. 'I'm sorry,' she whispered.

'I'm sorry, too,' he said. 'I had hoped to whisk you away and have you to myself, but it seems we're all going to Chinatown for a meal together. Is that all right with you?'

'Of course.' What else could she say?

The Chinese restaurant was a nice, cosy, old-fashioned one with crimson flock wallpaper and mahogany tables. Daniel managed to have them seated together in a discreet corner. Peter ordered a bottle of wine for the group, but Daniel was drinking water, and Kayleigh was amused when the waiter brought a brand that she was familiar with; she had done a lot of work for the company!

A waiter lit the candles and brought menus, and in time exquisitely pretty plates full of Chinese food started arriving. Kayleigh settled down to enjoy her meal, but then Fiona paused with a forkful in mid-air and said with considerable malice, 'If I ever go into politics like Daddy, I shall start a campaign against advertising. Most of it's unprincipled and downright dishonest!'

'Fiona!' Daniel barked warningly.

She looked indignant and grabbed the bottle of mineral water.

'It's true! Take this water – they spent millions on advertising it with pretty pictures of mountain streams, and in the end it turned out to be tap water.'

Daniel glared at Fiona. 'Kayleigh has nothing to do with that kind of advertising, do you, Kayleigh?'

Although she appreciated that he was supporting her, she smiled at him a little mischievously. 'I have actually been involved with this particular brand'

'You should be ashamed of yourself!' Fiona interrupted with a shriek.

Daniel's eyes opened wide in shock. 'Kayleigh, surely not?'

'Not with the first disastrous campaign,' she told him quickly. 'I handled the turnaround.'

'You?' said Fiona. 'But this water is produced by a huge multi-national. Why would they pay any attention to you?'

Kayleigh grinned. 'They were in such trouble, none of the big agencies wanted to know. So I sent the chief executive a cheeky proposal with my ideas for a rescue campaign, and she went for it!'

'I don't believe it!' Fiona snapped.

But Peter said, 'It's true. I was very impressed when I read about it in the business Press. Kayleigh was the only one who realised that, despite what the papers said, the company didn't ever sell ordinary tap water to the public. It was treated with exactly the same kind of technology as American astronauts use. Where they went wrong was in using the same branding as all the other bottled waters on the market, which gave the impression it was from a natural source. Fiona's right – it was dishonest, and it backfired, and once the Press got hold of the story their sales dropped to nothing.

'Of course,' Fiona said, satisfied that he was agreeing with her. 'People don't like being lied to.'

Peter nodded. 'That's why Kayleigh told the company to focus on the space-age technology and make it their unique selling point. It worked, too. The new black bottles and starry labels stand out from all the other brands, and sales are improving all the time.'

Daniel looked unimpressed. 'So a multi-national corporation gets to make more money. Who cares?'

Fiona looked satisfied by Daniel's reply, but his father gave him a pained look. 'Would you prefer a depression? A healthy market is better for everyone.'

'So you keep telling me!' Daniel replied casually.

Peter's eyes showed his hurt. 'You have never appreciated the benefits that the factory has brought you,' he said brusquely.

Suddenly Kayleigh realised that there were two sides to this argument: Peter might be critical, but Daniel was being equally dismissive. She was surprised that two intelligent people should be so stubborn, but when she looked at father and son carefully, she could see what strong chins they had, and what stern lines their lips could set in. There wasn't a penny to choose between them for obstinacy.

'The food at the Lucky Lantern is always delicious,' Ruth broke in loudly and clearly. 'Do you visit Chinatown often, Kayleigh?'

From then on Ruth kept the conversation so firmly locked on light topics that there was no chance for further argument about anything, and everyone was smiling as they collected their coats.

'It was lovely to see you, Daniel,' his

mother said, kissing the air above his cheek.

'It was a very pleasant evening. We won't leave it so long next time,' his father said. 'Your mother's abandoning me next month for a residential course. Perhaps we could get together then?'

'I'm having a little party on an evening when I know you're free, Daniel,' Fiona chimed in eagerly. 'Do come with your father.'

'Thanks, but on my next night off I'm hoping to persuade Kayleigh to have dinner with me.'

There was a short, charged silence as his family registered this. Peter Warner-Bond seemed unmoved by the news, while his wife looked cool but not distressed. However, Fiona's brows snapped together and she glared at Kayleigh with such venom that Kayleigh suddenly realised the woman was more interested in Daniel than in her chinless partner, and that she'd come out this evening for the sole purpose of meeting Daniel and asking him to her party.

But then Fiona turned away, saying goodbye to everyone so naturally that Kayleigh wondered if she was simply imagining things.

As she and Daniel walked back to the car,

though, she couldn't resist asking casually, 'Is Fiona a family friend?'

'Her father and mine were business partners once, so I've known her since she was a spotty girl.'

'She seems nice,' Kayleigh lied.

'She is very nice,' Daniel said. 'Her mother and mine get together every so often to make secret wedding plans, but I shall disappoint them in their dynastic scheming as I have in so much else.'

'Oh?' she enquired. They had reached the car. He pointed his key fob at it and the lights flashed and the doors clicked open.

'Fiona lives in a small patch of Cheshire where everyone has horses and a comfortable income and does nothing very much. I would die from boredom within a month,' he explained bluntly and Kayleigh could feel herself grinning as she sank into the comfort of his car.

This time she said nothing about cycling. They chatted about music as the big car purred through the streets to her home.

There was no space to park outside her house, so Daniel went a little way up the street and around the corner. When he switched off the engine, he turned to her with an engaging grin.

'Good. We're out of sight here.'

'Kevin'll have his binoculars out,' she teased.

'No use. Binoculars that can see round corners aren't on the market yet,' Daniel replied comfortably, turning in his seat to face her. 'Would you be happier if I were to walk you home now?'

Once again 'The Rules' went out the window. First date or not, she wanted to kiss him. He was gorgeous!

'Not just yet,' she murmured.

His arms went round her and pulled her close. He was warm and solid, and even in the awkward confines of a car, he felt just right. His blue eyes were smiling, and serious, too, as he moved to tenderly cup her face with his hands and lowered his lips to hers.

Kayleigh felt the same way she had when the opera had suddenly made sense, as if doors were blowing open in her heart and her mind.

They kissed for an age before he finally took his lips away. She snuggled her cheek into the crook of his neck and sighed because she was so happy.

Daniel stroked her hair with gentle fingers. 'Our first kiss,' he mused. 'We're connected now in a way that we weren't before.'

She sat up a little so that she could look into his eyes. 'You're very deep,' she commented.

'Do you mind?' he asked.

She shook her head. 'I like it. In fact–' But the ringing of his mobile phone ruined the moment.

Daniel sighed. 'My only night off this month. It had to happen.'

He answered the call quickly and came to a decision just as quickly.

'I'm on my way,' he told the caller, and hung up. He turned to Kayleigh. 'There's been an accident – an explosion. I'm sorry–'

'But you have to go,' she finished for him. 'Never mind, it's been a lovely evening.'

She stood on the doorstep until his car went by, then she went inside.

Her parents had gone to bed, and the house felt unnaturally tidy and quiet, the way it did when she came back from a holiday. She was glad none of her family was awake. In the morning, they would ask her how her date had been, and perhaps by the morning she would know how to answer them.

She crawled thankfully into the single bed that had been hers when she was at school and fell asleep at once.

Chapter Six

Ever Closer

Some time before dawn she came awake as completely as if someone had called her name. She could hear the birds singing and supposed it was the dawn chorus that had woken her.

She went to the kitchen for a drink of water, and on impulse opened the back door and stuck her head out into the cool air. The pear tree at the bottom of the garden made a beautiful silhouette against the dawn light, and a silver moon hung in one corner of the sky.

Now, if I were staging *Madame Butterfly*, I'd give everyone lovely Japanese costumes and a backdrop with a beautiful moon like that, she decided as she sipped her water, enjoying the magical way their tiny suburban garden had been transformed.

When she heard footsteps down the side of the house, her startled heart gave an extra beat, and she felt a moment's pure fear as a dark male figure came around the side of the house. But then she recognised him.

'Daniel?'

He was wearing the same clothes as when he had left her, but how different he looked. The joke tie was gone, and the crisp shirt was crumpled. He had grown a five o'clock shadow and he slouched as if he was so weary he could barely stand.

'Daniel!' she said again, concern sharpening her tone. 'What is it?'

He looked at her with such sad and shadowed eyes that she wanted to put her arms around him.

'What a night! There were so many casualties, you can't imagine. I did the best I could, but...'

'Come in,' Kayleigh said. 'Come in and sit down.'

He followed her obediently and sank into the family's squashy old sofa.

'You must think I'm crazy, coming here...'

A figure appeared in the doorway. 'Now then,' Mavis Hartley said, tying the belt of her old candlewick dressing-gown. Every Christmas the family gave her a new one, and every year she said thank you, put it in a cupboard, and continued to wear her favourite old one.

86

'I thought I heard voices,' she said.

'I'm sorry to have disturbed you, Mrs Hartley. I'll take myself off...'

'Don't be silly,' she replied. 'You hardly made a sound, but I'm a light sleeper.'

'Daniel had a bad night at the hospital,' Kayleigh explained.

'Then he'll be wanting a cup of tea and something to eat.'

'Oh, no, really, Mrs Hartley, I'm not at all hungry.'

'Daniel doesn't drink anything with caffeine in it, Mum.'

Mavis looked at her over Daniel's head and mouthed silently, 'Keep him awake,' then she vanished into the kitchen.

Kayleigh looked at the old clock on the mantelpiece and saw that it was half-past five.

'You've been up for hours,' she commented.

'To no good purpose,' he said grimly, staring at his feet. 'I feel so useless. I was so scared when I saw the first casualty.'

'*You* were scared? I didn't think doctors got scared.'

'I'm only a man who went to medical school – although on tonight's showing I'd say that I wasted my time there.'

'Did you do your best?' she asked him bluntly.

He lifted his head and looked into her eyes, his own dark and astonished.

'Of course.'

'Then stop beating yourself up,' she told him crisply. 'No one could ask any more.'

Mrs Hartley was back with the battered old tin tray that they all used when they were ill enough to have meals in bed.

'Scrambled eggs, and I've done you a nice Horlicks instead of tea.'

She stayed long enough to watch Daniel start eating like a starving man, and then tactfully left them alone again, and Kayleigh blessed her mother's good sense as she watched the colour come back into his face.

'Stay here,' she said. 'You're too tired to drive home.'

He yawned hugely and looked at her with drowsy, heavy eyes.

'That would be imposing on you too much. I must leave.'

'Just lie down on the sofa for a few minutes, then,' she pressed.

She left the room to find a spare duvet and when she came back he was fast asleep. She covered him tenderly, glad to see that his face looked peaceful again. Then she went back upstairs.

She met her mother on the landing. Mrs Hartley shook her head.

'He doesn't know it himself yet, but he loves you,' she said.

Kayleigh blinked in surprise. 'What makes you say that?'

'Came here like a homing pigeon, he did. Instinct, see – straight to you.'

'You fed him,' Kayleigh pointed out. 'Next thing you know, he'll be trying to pinch you off Dad.'

'Happen. But I think you know the truth. It was love at first sight, for him anyway,' Mrs Hartley said, looking at her with such love in her eyes that Kayleigh just had to hug her.

'He's a good man,' Mavis said, hugging the girl back. 'Anyone can see that. But it might not be plain sailing for the two of you. You're very different people from very different worlds.'

Daniel slept soundly until eleven o'clock on Saturday morning. The rest of the family tiptoed around him all morning, but then Kayleigh's nephew, Tommy, toddled up to him and pulled his nose.

'Man!' Tommy said.

'The man's tired, Tommy, leave him alone,' his mother whispered, but it was too late. Daniel's eyelids had flown open.

'Man!' Tommy declared again.

'Toddler!' a smiling Daniel said in reply. 'Good morning to you, young man.'

Tommy thought about it for all of a second, then he scrambled up on the sofa and got under the duvet, grinning.

'Bed!' he announced.

They made a touching picture, snuggled up together on the sofa, and Kayleigh couldn't help smiling as she brought Daniel a slice of lemon in hot water.

'I had no idea what you'd drink in the morning, but I thought this was safe enough,' she told him.

'I couldn't start the day without my mug of tea,' observed Bailey.

'Nor me,' Sandra put in. The couple had dropped in with Tommy on their way somewhere. 'In fact, I drink it all day. I couldn't do without my cup of tea.'

Now that Daniel was awake, the whole family soon congregated in the lounge, Charlene resting her leg in the reclined armchair, and Kevin switching on the TV.

Daniel smiled at Kayleigh as if they were alone. 'I drink a lot of herbal tea at home, but this is fine. Thank you.' For the drink and a lot more, said the message in his eyes. All the seats in the room were full, so Kayleigh sat on the floor next to Daniel.

'Will you come out with me today?' he asked. 'I was supposed to be heading off to a conference in Canada this morning, but I've missed my flight. So we could go to Paris for the day, if you like.'

'Paris? For a day?' she echoed.

'I'm sorry but I can't stay any longer – it's imperative that I attend the second day of the conference.'

'No, no – I meant that Paris is so far away. We can't go for just one day!'

'We can if we fly. I'd love to take you. It's such a romantic city.'

'And I would love to go, but I can't today. I'm going to a fundraiser later at Nanton with Bailey and Sandra, and then I've promised to baby-sit Tommy so that they can go out for a meal. It's their anniversary, you see.'

Bailey grinned at Daniel. 'Come with us to Nanton,' he invited cheerfully. 'It's not Paris, but it'll be fun, eh, Sands?'

Sandra smiled at Daniel. 'The more the merrier,' she coaxed.

How could he resist? In the end, he took

his car and insisted that Kayleigh travel with him. A tiny smile quirked his lips as he cast her a sideways glance.

'How fortunate that Tommy's baby seat took up so much room in their car. I like having you all to myself!'

A quick shave and a shower seemed to have restored him, and he looked rested and casual, wearing jeans and a sweater that he'd produced from the boot of his car. Last night might never have happened. Kayleigh looked at him doubtfully.

'What's wrong?' he asked, his eyes soft with concern.

'I was just thinking about the accident and how ... upset you were,' she confessed.

'I'm sorry. I shouldn't have burdened you with all that.'

'I didn't mean that. I'm just surprised that you seem so happy this morning.'

He shrugged. 'Doctors have to learn to compartmentalise their emotions. I've not forgotten, and I'm not unfeeling; it's more that I've cultivated the discipline of putting regrets behind me and moving on. One has to in order to be at one's best for the next patient.'

Kayleigh watched the traffic flowing past, and the rear end of Bailey and Sandra's familiar old car in front of them, rattling round the new ring road and through the black and white village of Nanton.

'I don't think I could do that,' she said finally.

'Don't worry about it. Which way do I turn here?'

'Follow Bailey...' she instructed, and they turned into a large field bordered with chestnut trees that was being used as a temporary car park.

Daniel seemed to enjoy helping put Tommy in his pushchair then they all set off for the fair.

'What a gorgeous day!' Sandra said, and it was. White clouds flew across the blue sky, whipped on by the same breeze that fluttered the coats and dresses of the people in the crowd. Kayleigh felt carefree, as if she were on holiday, too, and she could feel herself smiling as she looked up at Daniel, relishing his presence beside her.

'It's time for the duck race. It's a pound a go. Shall we all have one? It's a good cause.'

Daniel grinned. 'And what cause is it today?' he asked easily.

Kayleigh laughed. 'The badger tunnel, of course. We need another three thousand pounds before the council will order the work to start.'

Daniel seemed to freeze in his tracks, and looked around him, as if for the first time. The Cheshire field was filled with a fine mix of people. A girl with dreadlocks and a pierced nose ambled past them. Ladies in flowery frocks mingled with tattooed youths. But he didn't seem to notice the harmony.

'What's wrong?' she asked.

'Nothing.' The frost in his blue eyes suggested that he was unhappy, but if he wouldn't admit the fact, there was nothing she could do.

The sun shone as they walked down to the river where a young vicar was helping her friend Tom to sell tickets for the plastic ducks. Both men greeted Kayleigh with delight, though Tom's mouth dropped open in dismay when he recognised Daniel.

'It's OK!' she mouthed, and winked at him, but even as she said the words, she wondered if they were true. Daniel was an edgy presence next to her as they watched Sandra and Bailey choose their ducks.

A tall, thin man with fluffy white hair and a very pink face ambled over. He recognised Tom's blond surfer curls with evident delight.

'Hello there, young Thomas. I saw your

94

father at my club the other day. Looking very well, I thought, and so are you.' The tweed-clad aristocrat stood beaming gently at Tom, a complete contrast in his baggy shorts and Hawaiian shirt. 'How's the badger campaign coming along?'

'Not too bad, sir, thank you,' Tom said, grinning back. 'We only need to raise another three thousand pounds.'

'Splendid effort,' said the gent, and then he caught sight of Daniel.

'Mr Warner-Bond! My dear chap, how frightfully lucky to meet you.' He drew Daniel to one side, but his voice was still loud enough for everyone to hear. 'That chap of mine in Harley Street tells me I need an operation. I told him I want to talk to you first. Second opinion, that's the ticket.'

Daniel tactfully drew the man a little further away, smiled kindly, and bent his head to listen. Kayleigh watched with interest, noticing that Daniel soon had the older man's pink face wreathed in smiles.

'Oh, well, if you approve, old chap. I'll take the plunge,' the man told him.

When Daniel rejoined Kayleigh she was glad to see that he was more relaxed.

'Lord Wycoller is on the hospital board,' he told her, and it was as though his presence had given the event some sort of seal of approval.

Everybody stood on a beautiful arched stone bridge over the river to watch the duck race. As Kayleigh jumped up and down, screaming encouragement to duck number forty-four as it bobbed in the clear water, Daniel seemed to shake off his frost and yelled with the rest of them.

As duck number forty-four got caught up in an eddy of current and bobbed first over the finish line, Daniel swept Kayleigh off her feet in an exuberant bear hug.

Still laughing, the group strolled along to where the vicar and Tom were handing out prizes. Tom's eyes widened with alarm when he saw that Daniel was still with Kayleigh.

'Hey,' he said cautiously.

Daniel nodded amiably enough and said, 'Hello,' as he offered to carry the large hand-made plant-pot that was Kayleigh's prize, but she could see from his eyes that he didn't approve of the lad.

She was just wondering how much better or worse it would make the situation if she told Daniel about Tom's other two personas when she heard a child's shocked scream: 'Mummy!' Then there was a hubbub as the crowd gathered at the base of a tree, looking ominously at the ground.

Daniel reacted at once. Sensing an accident, he strode to the site. 'Let me through, please – I'm a doctor.'

As Kayleigh followed him, she could see a small crumpled figure lying on the grass under a tall cedar tree with wide low branches. Bright red blood jetted from the child's arm. A woman was standing over the prone toddler, her eyes big with shock.

Immediately Daniel clamped his right thumb over the wound to stem the flow and raised the child's arm up in the air, and Kayleigh could hear him talking encouragingly to him even as he was scanning the crowd urgently with his eyes.

'Call an ambulance,' he said, when his gaze found Kayleigh.

'Don't worry,' said the vicar, panting from his run across the field. 'Here comes the St. John Ambulance.'

The crowd parted helpfully as the vehicle nosed its way across the grass. Two attendants jumped out, followed by a woman in a tweed suit with a white coat over it. Her badge pronounced her the volunteer doctor.

'What happened?' she asked Daniel, and he quickly described the injury and the measures he had taken so far. The doctor nodded and gestured to one of the attendants.

'Bring me a dressing, would you?' Then she turned to Daniel. 'How shall we do the transfer?'

'On the count of three?' he suggested. She nodded and knelt down beside him, holding the dressing ready. 'One … two … three…' Daniel counted out, and in the blink of an eye the doctor had slapped on the dressing and was holding it in place.

She turned to Daniel with admiration in her eyes. 'Great job – thanks. Do you want to come to the hospital with us?'

He shook his head. 'I don't know the family – I was just in the right place at the right time.'

Once the child had been transferred to the ambulance, he rejoined Kayleigh. Sandra and Bailey rushed over to them both, looking startled at the amount of blood on his clothes.

'I'll have to get changed,' he commented. 'Luckily I've got more clothes in my car.'

'What happened exactly?' Bailey asked.

'I'm guessing the little lad slipped away from his mother and decided to try his hand at tree climbing. But he fell and got caught by a branch or something that tore his arm open. Nasty.'

Sandra was very pale. 'Will he be all right? He was such a tiny scrap.'

'I think so,' Daniel answered. 'We got to him before he'd lost too much blood.'

'*You* did, you mean! Little boys are like quicksilver – that's why I make Tommy stay in his pushchair. If he's not strapped in, he's off into trouble before I can stop him.'

Kayleigh went with Daniel back to his car, where he pulled a big sports bag out of the boot.

'I always keep some changes of clothes here,' he explained. 'Doctors can get dirtier than car mechanics on occasion, and a spare set comes in handy. As for these – they're only fit for the bin now. There should be some rubbish bags in here somewhere...'

She found the roll of plastic garbage sacks, but when she bent to pick up the blood-stained garments, her skin went cold, blackness clouded her vision and a roaring like a giant waterfall filled her ears.

'Daniel...' she said faintly.

He was by her side in a second, strong arms supporting her. 'The sight of all that blood has upset you. Here – take a seat in the car. Good. Now put your head down – right down...'

The faintness soon passed.

'I'm OK now,' she said, straightening up and shaking her hair back.

He was kneeling on the ground before her, his blue eyes scrutinising every inch of her face. His whole being radiated astonishment.

'Daniel, what is it?'

'I think I'm falling in love with you,' he answered quietly.

She looked deep into his eyes for another long moment, aware now that she must be looking as surprised as he was. A warmth stole over her, but she felt shy as well. Love? It was a big word, and a scary concept. She had never been in love, and she felt vulnerable and uncertain.

It was a relief to hear a distant shout as Tommy hurtled towards them followed by Bailey and Sandra.

It had already been arranged that Daniel and Kayleigh would take Tommy back with them while Sandra and Bailey went off for their anniversary celebration.

'Have a lovely time,' Kayleigh urged, giving Sandra a warm hug. 'Don't hurry back. Tommy will be fine with us. With me, I mean.' She blushed but Sandra tactfully ignored it – or maybe she didn't notice. Her dark eyes were soft with memories.

'The Silver Trout is my favourite hotel in all the world. When we got married, we couldn't afford a honeymoon abroad, but they looked after us ever so well there.'

'Well, enjoy your meal,' Kayleigh repeated.

She waved them off, then turned back to Daniel, whose eyes weren't meeting hers. Shyness constricted her throat. There was so much unsaid between them.

As the luxurious car purred along the motorway, a deep, mysterious happiness that she didn't care to examine too closely welled up in her, but she knew that she was happier than she had ever been in her life.

Once they got back to the house, Tommy's tea-time, bath-time and bed-time kept them busy. Daniel was good with the toddler, and could provoke gales of laughter from him, but Kayleigh was glad to see that he also knew when to stop.

'I think it's time for a nice, quiet bed-time story, young man,' he finally declared and was rewarded with an adorable grin.

Daniel sat on the side of the child's bed while Kayleigh perched at the foot, and they took it in turns to read to him until his eyelids drooped.

'Little cherub,' Kayleigh whispered as she

tiptoed to the door.

Daniel's expression was wistful. 'I hadn't realised how fulfilling time spent with a child could be.' His voice was a murmur that might have been for himself alone.

Downstairs, Bill Hartley was comfortably ensconced in front of the television in the oldest of his fishing sweaters and a pair of thick socks.

'It's just me,' he said. 'Kevin's out with his mates and the missus has pushed Charlene's wheelchair round to see our neighbour, Beverley. Her daughter's getting married, you know.'

'And Mrs Hartley is doing the cake?' Daniel guessed.

'That's right. She does a good cake, my missus. Now then, I hear you don't drink tea. Can I get you a Horlicks – and a sand-wich, maybe?'

'Thank you. I am hungry, as it happens. Egg soldiers for tea don't seem to sustain me through the evening the way they did when I was two.'

Kayleigh's hand flew to her mouth. 'I'm sorry! I've been neglecting you! Don't worry about it, Dad, I'll make Daniel something.'

'I don't want to put you to the trouble of cooking. I could ring for a takeaway? Do

102

you like Chinese food, Mr Hartley?'

'I can't say as I care for it, son, but I've had my tea anyway. Any road, it's Saturday night – you two should get yourself off out. I don't need your help to mind little Tommy.'

'Are you sure, Dad?' Kayleigh asked, and he was insistent.

As they drove into the city centre, Daniel looked down at his old jeans and fleece pullover. 'I'm not very presentable. Maybe I should go home to get changed first?'

'What about me?' she protested. 'I can't go to a restaurant looked this scruffy any more than you can. Shall I go back and change, too?'

Daniel hesitated and then said, 'How do you feel about that takeaway after all? There's a good Chinese near my house.'

She cast a quick glance at his face, but in her heart she knew she could trust him.

'I'd love to. I'm dying to see your house.'

'I hope you won't be disappointed,' he said. 'It's pretty boring. I spend so little time there, you see.'

Daniel's house was brand new, on an executive estate, with a huge garden and double garage, but it was dull. Although it was spotlessly clean and the furniture was new, it had the unmistakably forlorn air of a bachelor pad. Kayleigh was secretly delighted that there was no evidence of a girlfriend ever having been there.

'It needs a woman's touch,' she pronounced.

'A delightful young lady called Jan comes round every Thursday to clean,' Daniel protested, but the twinkle in his eye showed that he understood her meaning. 'I bought the house in a hurry when I took this appointment, purely because it was near the hospital. I've never had time to think about making it more homely.'

They piled the Chinese food cartons on the coffee table and Kayleigh warmed a couple of plates. Daniel smiled.

'It's nice to be eating at home with you like this. I hope you don't mind not going out to a restaurant?'

'Of course not. And this is delicious,' she said, licking her fingers.

'The Golden Lotus's food never lets me down,' he commented.

Once they'd finished, he opened the final packet.

'Fortune cookies! What fun!' Kayleigh cried. 'Read yours first.'

'No, yours!' Daniel insisted, and then he

read it out loud for her. '"Young woman who travel will get great good fortune".'

'Travel? What a shame – I'm not planning any trips.'

'Let's read mine. Hm – "Doctor who go to Canada alone very unfortunate".' He looked up and his eyes met hers. 'I'll have to go tomorrow. My plane is at five in the morning. Will you come with me?'

'To Canada?' she said blankly.

'I *have* to attend the second day of the conference; I'm presenting a paper – one I have worked rather hard on, I might add. But it would make me very happy if you would consider accompanying me. We would be back on Friday afternoon.'

The siren call to adventure was playing in her heart and mind, but she couldn't quite bring herself to answer it.

Daniel leant forward and took her hand, his blue eyes intimate.

'I would love to take you with me. Toronto's a beautiful city. I want to watch your eyes when I show you the wonders of the new world. I want to take you to a romantic little restaurant where we can talk for hours. I want to listen to more of that beautiful laugh of yours. I want to be with you so that we can get to know one another.'

His eyes searched her face. She could see that he was sincere, and decided that he deserved the truth.

'It's too soon. It's too much. Oh, I meant to say it better than that, but, Daniel, you're so serious that you frighten me a little.'

She felt more for him than she had ever felt for a man before, but she refused to be rushed.

'I do like you, Daniel, so much, but we only met last week.'

As he lifted her hand and kissed it, Kayleigh felt her breath catch, and she didn't know whether to be glad or sorry when he let it go.

'My dating skills must have gone rusty,' he said ruefully. 'When I was in medical school I used to be so polished, so on top of it, and now I'm apparently so inept that I've frightened you away!'

Kayleigh grinned at him. 'Oh, no, you haven't! I want to see you when you come back. Anyway, what makes you think a calculated seduction would work on me? I like my men natural.'

His eyes lit up with amusement and he laughed.

'You are a darling! I'll be looking forward to our next date the whole time I'm away.'

Chapter Seven

Differing Views

Kayleigh and Daniel talked a lot on the phone over the next week, and he sent unexpectedly cute texts.

When he got back they still couldn't meet because of his packed schedule, so they carried on talking by phone. On Monday, while they were chatting at lunch-time, he mentioned his workload.

'I've instructed my secretary to scale down my operating list. I didn't realise what an insane schedule I was working until I wanted to take time out to meet you. I'm sorry but this week I truly can't get away before seven-thirty on Friday.'

'That's fine by me, but you'll be exhausted if you've worked all day.'

'I think I can promise to stay awake for you!' he returned.

Kayleigh couldn't remember the last time she'd looked forward to a date so eagerly. She worked hard all week, as always, but in between clients was the delicious awareness of her relationship with Daniel and a pleasurable excitement that grew and blossomed as Friday got closer.

She finished work promptly at five on Friday, but the very second her hand touched the door handle to leave, her boss called her back.

'Kayleigh, could you come into my office, please?'

Nick Cornish was very smart in suit, collar and tie, and his dark eyes held a severe expression. There was a print-out of an email on his desk.

'Is this your handiwork?' he asked.

Kayleigh scanned it briefly. 'Yes.'

'Well, I have to tell you that I don't approve of the tone.' He picked it up. 'A client contacted you to say that the promotional campaign run by my company had resulted in a fifty per cent increase in business for her hairdressing salon, and you replied, "YAY! SMOKING HOT SCISSORS!" I hardly see that as being an appropriate response.'

'Tracy's my best friend,' she explained. 'It wasn't a problem.'

'I disagree. The tone of your communication is completely inappropriate. You should have replied expressing your satisfaction and offering to sell the client another service, for the full price this time, I might add. Joan was far too liberal with discounts.

'I also dislike the coloured font and silly animations you use on your communications. In future I would ask you to use the house style with no embellishments, and to address clients formally. Would it be so difficult to call your client Miss Bradshaw?'

'Well ... I'm much more formal with clients that I have a business relationship with, but I went to school with Tracy.'

'Don't argue with me,' he snapped, scowling, and as she met his eyes she saw nothing but rancour in them.

'Nick, I respect your point of view–' she began.

'Then darned well adhere to it. Now get out!'

Kayleigh felt stirred up all the way home. She didn't like the changes Nick was making on a professional level, and today's little interview told her that he was bearing a grudge because she had turned down a date with him when he had first arrived.

Her mind was busy as she showered and dried her hair. Was she going to have to find a new job?

It wasn't until she sat in front of her dressing-table and started applying her make-up that she got a thrill down to her toes as she remembered that Daniel was waiting for her.

The supper club where she was meeting him was warm, dark and mysterious. From the doorway, Kayleigh saw Daniel waiting at a round table, and as she made her way towards him, he jumped to his feet, his handsome face full of anxiety. 'I was so worried about you!'

She glanced at her watch. She was ten minutes late.

'I'm sorry. I got held up at work.'

'What happened?'

'I'll tell you in a minute. Just let me take off my coat.'

The club was full of heat and atmosphere, with tiny tables clustered around a small circular dance floor. All of the flowers and decorations had an African flavour, and the air was rich with exotic spices. Although the club specialised in live music, the musicians were taking a break, their drums cast to one side.

'This is lovely!' Kayleigh said, looking around with real pleasure.

However Daniel's eyes showed that he was still upset. 'I rang you but you didn't answer your phone!'

Her hand flew to her mouth. 'Sorry! I had a meeting and forgot to turn it back on!'

She rummaged in her bag and turned on her phone. Sure enough, there were three voice messages and two texts, all from Daniel. The first one was timed at five past five that evening.

'My last surgery was cancelled,' he explained. 'I was hoping to reach you in case you were able to meet me early.'

His eyes still showed a trace of anxiety he'd been feeling, and she tried to lighten the mood. 'So you've been trying to reach me for hours. No wonder you're in such a state,' she said with a laugh.

His eyebrows snapped together. 'I'm not in a state! I was concerned in case there had been an accident.'

She was about to tell him how unlikely that was, but then she remembered his job. He was all too aware that accidents could and did happen regularly. Why, they would never even have met that fateful third time if not for Charlene's own accident.

So she smiled and reached out to hold his hand across the table. 'I'm sorry you were worried, but I'm here now, and this place is lovely. Let's enjoy ourselves.'

Daniel had a non-alcoholic cocktail while

Kayleigh chose a splash of rum in a glass of exotic fruit juice. She swirled her drink so that the ice tinkled and then reached over to chink her glass against his.

'Cheers!' She giggled, and was relieved to see the tight lines around his eyes relax a little at last.

The décor was magical, but the food at dinner was a mixed success.

'I see you've left your meat,' Daniel noted. 'Is it just alligator you object to, or do you refuse to eat any meat on principle?'

'I don't eat much meat as it happens. But I did try it.'

He smiled. 'Shall we try a dance now?'

The musicians were beating out soft, rhythmic music, and Kayleigh felt perfectly happy as Daniel took her in his arms. She fitted beneath his chin as if his shoulder had been made to support her.

They danced in silence for a while, and then he bent his head to kiss her lips, and Kayleigh felt her breathing change in response to him.

He drew back, just far enough to search her eyes, and she wondered what he could read there. She could read desire in his, but she was used to that. Many men desired her for her looks, but what about her soul? She had never come close to finding a soulmate before, but she wondered if he might be the one.

He kissed her soft bare neck. She could feel his breath tickling her skin. The warmth sent delicious little shivers down her spine.

They still didn't say a word, but danced on in glorious soft intimacy, moving to the rhythm of the drums that beat in the darkness.

When the lights went up Kayleigh was surprised. 'They must close early here. What time is it?'

Daniel grinned. 'It's two in the morning,' he told her, and laughed at her amazement. The time had flown! 'Time to take you home.'

As they drove along, she stared out of the car window at the dark streets. She hadn't expected the love of her life to be a man who was so different from her.

She cast a glance at him as he drove steadily through the night, his gaze concentrated on the road. The strong planes of his face were calm. His professional control was part of what was different about him, but it was part of his attraction as well. He was passionate, but she could trust him. She had never known a man who seemed as mature as Daniel.

She sighed contentedly as they neared her home and he glanced at her.

'Everything all right?' he asked.

'Yes. I was just thinking.'

'You never told me what happened to delay you earlier.'

Kayleigh smiled as she remembered the tiresome Nick. His behaviour seemed so petty when she looked back on it.

'There's trouble at work. I don't like my new boss.'

His sympathy seemed to evaporate. 'Sometimes the best bosses have to do things that aren't popular.'

'But you don't know what he's done!'

'Has he found out that you moonlight as an eco-warrior?'

'No. Goodness knows how he'd react if he did!'

'I think he'd be justified in his concern,' he commented, and she turned to stare at him.

'What do you mean?'

'Well – you mix with some odd people. You should be more careful.'

'And let the badgers die?'

'I'm not saying it's not a good cause, but I think you should stop getting involved in direct action. You could get into trouble.'

'What sort of trouble?'

'You had a loaded gun pointed at you just last week!'

'But I care about the environment.'

'Then make a donation to an organised group.'

Kayleigh heard the irritation in his voice, but she didn't intend to let him criticise her just because she was passionate about the matter.

'You're being a complete and utter idiot!' she snapped, and he looked so astonished that she almost laughed. 'What? Don't they answer you back at the hospital? Well, I certainly will. If you think I'm so much trouble, why do you want to spend time with me?'

His lips were unforgiving as he said, 'You don't fit in with that bunch of weirdos. You're beautiful, successful and talented.'

Kayleigh wouldn't soften. 'If you can't accept *both* sides of me, then we're history.'

He drove on without saying another word.

As usual, there was no room to park outside her parents' house, so he drove around the corner and halted the big car under a streetlight. Kayleigh sat next to him, wondering what his next move would be. She couldn't predict his reaction: another outburst or a cool, cutting remark?

She waited. He sat in silence, looking straight ahead. Still she waited, for what seemed like a lifetime, although it was only a few minutes by the dashboard clock. A clock that was showing after two-thirty in the morning.

'Daniel, it's late,' she finally said.

He stirred and turned to her, his face serious. 'I apologise,' he began. 'I'm truly sorry.'

Kayleigh was aware of a deep sense of relief. She knew then how afraid she had been that she would lose him.

'I don't understand why I was so critical,' he went on. 'It was thoroughly uncalled for. Can you forgive me?' he asked softly.

'Of course.'

An alarm beeped in his pocket, and he reached in to turn it off without looking at it, his gaze never leaving her face.

'I should go now – I've got to catch a flight to Frankfurt – but I don't like to leave you with this unresolved.'

'Our quarrel's over,' she promised him. 'How long are you away for?'

'Just three days. I go every month, to teach at a hospital there. It was a great honour to be invited, but I think I'll resign.' He touched her cheek gently. 'You've made me realise that I do nothing but work.'

'All that work is what got you to the top,' she pointed out. 'I've looked you up on the Internet. You're world class!'

He seemed unmoved by her compliments. His eyes scanned her face urgently. 'Will you wait for me? Will you see me when I come back?'

'You bet your sweet life I will,' she promised.

It wasn't hard to wait for Daniel. Her looks attracted as many offers as ever, but Kayleigh turned them all down. Other men were pale shadows compared with him, yet the way he viewed their relationship with such serious intensity was overwhelming, and rather frightening. Or was it the intensity of her own response that frightened her? She wished she could talk to someone about her feelings.

In fact, she arranged to meet her best friend Tracy after work on Friday with the specific purpose of talking things over. They met up in their usual little cappuccino bar near Tracy's beauty salon, and talked of nothing in particular for about an hour while the espresso machine steamed noisily in the background. There was music playing, too, and as she recognised one track Kayleigh felt nostalgic.

'I never hear this rock and roll anywhere but here. It always makes me think of exchanging secrets with you.'

Tracy leaned back and opened her china-blue eyes very wide.

'You're not telling me much today!'

'There's nothing to tell,' Kayleigh said, finding herself completely unable to discuss the very feelings she had planned to talk about.

Tracy looked at her and grinned. 'No? *Someone's* put that dreamy expression in your eyes!'

Now was the time to spill out her feelings and maybe get some advice, but Kayleigh found herself struck dumb. Tracy watched her for a moment longer, then smiled.

'I've never yet dated a man that I couldn't tell you about. The fact that you don't want to talk about Daniel tells me everything.'

Kayleigh shifted uneasily in her seat and looked down at her coffee cup. She was still trying to sort out her feelings, when Tracey's fabulous manicured hand brushed hers lightly.

'It's OK, I'll stop teasing you now. Did I

tell you I tried speed dating last week?'

'No!' Kayleigh looked up, grinning, blessing Tracy for letting her off the hook. 'Tell me all about it!'

They chatted on until it was time to go, hugging warmly as they parted. Kayleigh and Tracy would always be friends, she knew, but on a different level now. The gap that had opened up between them was all a part of the strangeness of her life since she'd met Daniel. There had never been anything she couldn't share with her best friend before.

When Daniel came back from Frankfurt he had a full operating list, and then he was due for a quick trip to Jersey. They talked for an hour most evenings, but Daniel was exceptionally disciplined about not going out the night before a full day at the hospital.

'I can't afford to make a mistake,' he said. 'Not now one's operating statistics are published on the Internet. It would ruin my record.'

'That was a joke, right?' Kayleigh asked, wishing she could see his face.

How she loved his deep, dark laugh. 'Of course it's not a joke. I'm very proud of my record.'

'You're still teasing me, I know you are.'

'I wish I was kissing you,' he murmured, and she fell silent, listening to his soft, faraway breathing.

'Oh, Daniel, when will I see you?'

'Thursday evening. And then we'll have a long weekend.'

However, first thing on Thursday morning she had a phone call that astonished her. From a recruitment consultant.

'We hear you might be persuaded to consider a new position,' said the confident, rather plummy voice. 'My clients think a great deal of you. Can I persuade you to meet with them?'

'Of course. How about after work tonight?' Kayleigh offered.

The city centre hotel where they were to meet had a splendid marble entrance at which she was greeted by a uniformed doorman who ushered her into a private lounge. A middle-aged English woman with a pleasant expression and salt and pepper hair greeted her, as did a younger American woman who shone with gloss and grooming.

As Kayleigh took the offered chair, the American smiled. 'So this is the woman who turned round that disastrous bottled water campaign. The Marsh-Shaw agency in New

York is expanding. How would you feel about joining the team there? My employers are convinced that you have the kind of creativity they're looking for.'

Kayleigh sat back in her seat. 'Wow!' she said, shaking her head. 'It's very kind of you, but I hadn't ever thought of moving to the States.'

'You might when you see the package we're offering,' the American told her.

She was almost right. When Kayleigh got home, she leafed through the job description and the relocation details. The lavish salary the Americans were offering made her glow; it was the best compliment to her professional competence she had ever received. It made her so happy to be judged by her performance and not by her beauty.

Her parents were impressed and delighted, and immediately rang Bailey and Sandra to tell them the news. Then Kayleigh rang Tracy who squealed like a teenager. It was all joy until she told Daniel at the restaurant that evening. He barely looked up from the menu.

'Oh, Americans – what do they know about anything?'

Kayleigh eyed him with surprise. 'But it's such a compliment!'

He shrugged. 'It annoys me the way those American head-hunters hang around the hospital like jackals. As soon as someone gets a basic qualification, out comes a fancy job offer. Are you ready to order yet?'

The way he was brushing aside her feelings hurt. 'Daniel–' she began, but the waiter was upon them to take their orders.

As soon as he had gone, Daniel reached across the table to take her hands. 'I've missed you so much.'

Kayleigh met the ardour in his blue eyes and realised that he was on a completely different wavelength. He had no idea that he had upset her and she had no idea how to tell him.

As he continued to examine her face in the way that was so characteristic of him, a shadow clouded his eyes. 'What's wrong, sweetheart? You don't look happy.'

She chose her words carefully. 'I was pleased to be head-hunted because it means the Americans think I'm smart.'

He laughed. 'Too smart to go to America, I hope.'

'I appreciated the offer.'

'You wouldn't like working in America. It wouldn't be right for you. As for the offer, they're ten-a-penny – I get them all the time.'

'*You might* get them all the time,' Kayleigh tried to explain, 'but I don't. Of course I'm taking it seriously.'

'Kayleigh, you can't go to America. It would be all wrong for you.'

'Can't?' she repeated ominously. 'Just listen to yourself.'

She could see a thunder storm gathering in his eyes.

'One of us has to have some sense,' he said. 'America isn't the right environment for you. You really shouldn't go.'

'You have no right to tell me what to do.'

'Well, I want that right, Kayleigh – to advise you, at least. So I'd better marry you.'

She stared at him in blank amazement, and he grinned. 'I didn't mean to blurt it out like that, but I do want to marry you.'

She stared at him, at his handsome face and his glossy dark hair. He was the most gorgeous man she had ever met and she adored him. But marriage? She really didn't know the first thing about him.

'I've taken you by surprise,' Daniel said, and took her hand again. 'I know I'm rushing you, but let's get engaged. I want everyone to know that we belong together. I want to make plans for the future.'

'But – it's crazy! We only met last month.'

'We had our first date five weeks ago. That's long enough for me to know that I love you. You're the most stunning woman I've ever known. I love you and I want to be with you for ever.' He laughed ruefully. 'I was planning such a careful seduction, and here I am blurting out my proposal over the dinner table. But, Kayleigh, your beautiful face takes my breath away. As soon as I see you I want you so badly that all my common sense blows away with the wind.'

He captured her fingers in his hand. 'What are you thinking, Kayleigh? Do you care for me at all? Shall we get engaged?'

She raised her gaze to his and listened to her heart, and joy suffused his face the second their eyes met. Her expression must have told him what he wanted to know even before she spoke.

'It might be nice,' she said.

Daniel's grin was huge. 'We're going to be so happy,' he promised. 'Now, let's get out of here so that I can kiss you!'

Chapter Eight

The Most Beautiful Day...

Daniel picked up Kayleigh early the next morning for the excursion they had planned to the countryside. He was conservatively dressed in a waxed jacket and corduroy trousers, and looked taken aback when he saw her clothes.

'You're not planning to go to any demonstrations today, are you?'

She gave him a twirl and a little tap dance to show off her big boots.

'Don't you like me in green? I go fishing with Dad sometimes; this is what I wear to keep warm.'

He put his arms around her embroidered padded jacket and hugged her soundly, rubbing the tip of his nose against hers.

'It's a bit like trying to kiss an Eskimo!' he laughed. 'But I suppose it is on the chilly side today. In fact, I had thought that you might want to abandon our walk and go shopping for an engagement ring instead.'

'A ring?' Kayleigh said, pausing as she got into the car and meeting his sparkling eyes over its roof. He gave her a huge smile and she had to wonder if life got any better.

'I know a fabulous jeweller, and she's keeping a selection of rings in reserve for you.'

Kayleigh wasn't a bit sorry when a splatter of cold rain hit the windscreen.

'We could go shopping first,' she suggested cheerfully. 'Oh, but I'd better get changed first. I can't go like this.'

'You don't have to worry what you wear to visit Yao Ming's shop.' He cast an anxious look at her. 'I hope you like the place. He was going to die on me, you see, and the only way I could get him to hang on was to promise him that I would buy my engagement ring from his shop.'

'He was one of your patients?'

'A very stubborn one!' Daniel laughed, taking the road for Chinatown. 'He had me worried for a while, but he pulled through.'

'Do you keep in touch with many of your patients?' she asked.

'Very few,' he answered. 'But sometimes friendships spring up.'

Daniel parked by a gilded dragon then took her down a non-descript alley and stopped by a green painted door. The bronze door handle was in the shape of a dragon. He knocked loudly.

Mr Yao smiled when he opened the door and saw him, and looked even more delighted when he saw Kayleigh with him.

'You not come for a mah-jong lesson today?' he teased Daniel.

'Not today. I still want to learn how to play the game,' Daniel told the old man, 'but I have so little free time.'

Mr Yao led them along a dark corridor that smelt of spices and smoke.

'Three times in six years you visit me. Not enough to learn rules,' he grumbled mildly.

Kayleigh wondered what on earth she was letting herself in for. She imagined a dusty Chinese shop full of junk and forgotten treasures; what kind of rings might the old man stock? But once she was in the room all her doubts fell away.

The room was vast, bright and modern. Spotlights shone down from the ceiling to be reflected in the polished wooden floor. Glass glittered and shone around the modern display cases, while a bold sculpture made of twisted neon tubes glowed in the centre of the room. And the jewellery! The room was full of treasures.

A slim Chinese woman wearing a very smart suit came to greet her.

'Jade Snow Yao, my second cousin's daughter.' Mr Yao introduced her with pride. 'Jade is top designer always in the glossy magazines.'

Jade's black eyes were smiling. 'That's enough, Uncle! Hello, Kayleigh. Daniel described you perfectly – I think you're going to like the ring he selected for you. Come and see it.'

As Jade unlocked a display case, Daniel spoke with a trace of nervousness that Kayleigh found endearing. 'You can have any ring you like. If you think this one's awful, you must say so. In fact, now that I look at it again, I'm not sure it's good enough for you.'

The ring slipped on to her finger as if it was made for her. It was a simple gold band with one large diamond and a cluster of smaller diamonds floating around it. The design was clean, modern, perfectly simple, and yet it had the unmistakable air of a work of art.

'I love it,' Kayleigh breathed. 'Oh, Daniel!'

She turned to look at him and the love in his eyes made her heart overflow with emotion so that tears welled in her eyes.

Jade slid open a glass door that led out to a tiny courtyard and gestured to a stone bench overlooking a goldfish pond.

'Sit here for a minute. I'll make you some jasmine tea.'

It was a chilly July day with grey clouds scudding across the sky and a scatter of raindrops in the wind, but Kayleigh had never felt so happy.

'You'll be cold,' Daniel said anxiously, following her out.

'We're dressed for it,' she reminded him, looking down at her padded jacket and boots. 'Though this isn't how I imagined being dressed when I wore my engagement ring for the very first time!'

He put his arms around her and she snuggled into the warmth of him.

'We can do it again, if you like,' he told her. 'Somewhere more romantic.'

Kayleigh lifted her head to gaze around the tiny courtyard, at the golden fish that flickered in the lily pool, at the big stone statues of Chinese temple dogs that guarded some red gates in one corner. Tall clumps of potted bamboo rustled in the wind. Jade came towards them with fine china cups full of golden tea, but as soon as she had placed the tray on a table, she slipped tactfully away again and left them alone.

'Nothing could be more romantic than this!' Kayleigh declared. All her hurt feelings from the night before had evaporated in the charm of the moment. Her doubts vanished. 'Oh, Daniel, I'm so happy!'

He kissed her then, and as they drank the jasmine tea Kayleigh admired the sparkle of her ring in natural light.

'It looks as if the sun's going to make an appearance after all,' Daniel said, looking up at the sky. 'Shall we try for that walk? I've booked us lunch at the Green Swan, and there's a very pleasant circuit around the river and through the woods at the back of it.'

'Oh, I know it around there,' Kayleigh said. 'Dad fishes there sometimes. He's caught some lovely trout.'

'You'll be familiar with the pub then. The food's superb.'

'Not really. We usually take butties and a flask!' she confessed, thinking again what a different lifestyle Daniel had.

On the way to the Green Swan, Kayleigh asked him to stop the car, and took him round a bend in a long winding farm track to show him a farmhouse sitting in a snug hollow beneath the green hills. A substantial trout stream winked in the sunlight on the left side of the farm.

'This is my mum and dad's dream house,' she told him.

'It's a nice little place,' he said. 'And look, it's for sale. Shall we walk down and check it out?'

As they crunched down the gravel farm track, Kayleigh looked at him curiously. 'What kind of a house did you grow up in, Daniel?'

'The family home is very old. It's in Cheshire, but you know that. It was built by my great-grandfather from the proceeds of the original bicycle factory and we haven't changed it much, although we have put in central heating and a couple of bathrooms.'

'How big is it?' she asked, trying to picture it.

'It's quite a decent size, I suppose. In fact, it's a bit too big for modern life. It has stables and a granary, and there are a couple of farms. We rent those out. I suppose the land adds up to five-hundred-odd acres in total. A few years ago some nearby pasture and a lake came up for sale, so my father bought them to prevent anyone building on them. We can see the lake from the house, and he didn't want the view being spoilt.'

'It must have been amazing growing up in such luxury.'

'It seemed normal to me since I'd never known anything else, and plenty of my friends had bigger places.'

'Where did you go to school?'

She wasn't surprised when he named the top private school in the area. No wonder he seemed different – he *was* different. And when he said the farm they were standing in front of was an nice little place, he meant that, too. By his standards, it *was* a little place, yet all her life the Hartley family had dreamed of this farm as the ultimate luxury.

It was empty, so they wandered around the yard and garden and peeped in all the windows of the cosy, honey-coloured stone house.

'It's perfect,' she sighed. 'It's only been on the market once before, when I was about five years old. We all got very excited, but the price – well, it was out of the question.'

Daniel didn't seem to register the fact that the property was unaffordable for her family.

'You should tell your father that it's back on the market.'

'Umm,' she said noncommittally as they

turned to go back to the car.

At the bend in the farm track, Daniel halted and pulled her to him, his eyes sparkling with fun and love, and she wound her arms around his neck and kissed him hungrily. His kiss was as potent as a cocktail.

'I love you so much, Kayleigh.'

For the first time, she said it back: 'I love you, too.'

So then, of course, he kissed her again, and in the end they only had time for quite a short walk before their lunch booking.

Kayleigh looked around at the cosy décor of the pub dining-room and sighed contentedly. 'You take me to the nicest places.'

'I want to spend my whole life taking you to nice places and making you happy!' he said earnestly.

After the meal they went into the lounge bar, where a log fire roared in a stone fireplace and the bar glittered and shone with polished glass. Tapestry cushions softened the dark oak chairs, and they managed to get two in a corner. Daniel brought Kayleigh a delicious liqueur coffee.

'You miss out on so much,' she remarked sadly, wishing he could share in her pleasure in the drink. He was having a soda water himself.

'A few sacrifices are necessary if one is to achieve one's ambition.'

'True,' she answered, thinking of the challenges she had faced at work.

He looked into her eyes. 'What would you say your major ambition is?'

Her thoughts went to the dream farmhouse, and she imagined being able to buy it for her parents.

'I want to earn a million pounds–' she began, but to her amazement Daniel didn't wait to hear the rest of her dream.

He drew back and surveyed her with an air of disdain. 'That hardly fits with your expressed desire to save the planet,' he commented.

She felt as she had missed her step and fallen into a hole full of ice water. She wished she could go back to the rosy glow of only a few moments ago, but she couldn't escape the truth. She put down her coffee cup slowly, hot, painful regret clawing at her heart.

'What? What is it?' Daniel asked.

'You didn't even let me finish my sentence,' she said slowly.

'I'm sorry. What were you going to say?'

She bit her lip, feeling a creeping cold in the very core of her being as she took off her engagement ring and laid it on the table.

His expression was astounded. 'Why?' he demanded. 'Why?'

'It's too soon to get engaged,' she told him. 'We don't know one another well enough for such a commitment.'

'But I love you!'

She met the passion and the love in his eyes and felt nothing but certainty as she pushed the ring towards him.

'I want a million pounds so that I can buy the farm we just looked at for my parents. My only interest in money is using it to make the people I love happy. I also want the kind of husband who would know that about me.'

'I'm sorry, but *I* didn't know what you wanted the money for.'

'You *should* have known,' she told him frankly. 'I need a husband who'll be on my side, who'll believe in me and support me no matter what. I think we have issues to work out between us yet. You like my face, Daniel, but do you like *me?* You don't like my activism, do you?'

'No,' he admitted. 'But wouldn't you give it up if we were married?'

'No.'

'But that's ridiculous. You're only one

person, Kayleigh you can't make that much difference.'

'The Dalai Lama says that anybody who thinks they're too small to make a difference has never spent a night with a mosquito.'

He shrugged and reached for her hands. 'How is this important to us?' he asked, but she firmly drew her hands from his grasp.

'Don't brush my feelings aside, Daniel.'

His eyes were bright and very confident. 'I know you care about your badgers, but surely even you can see how odd some of the people in the campaign are?'

'I know some of them have extreme views, but I have some very good friends in the group. We're not all the same, you know, any more than doctors are.'

'Doctors have to work hard to earn the title. Anyone can protest,' he snapped back.

Kayleigh met his eyes boldly. 'Would you let me use our house as a base for the badger campaign?'

He looked distinctly uncomfortable and she knew the answer.

'Daniel, I can't be engaged to somebody who doesn't approve of my activities or my friends,' she said, getting to her feet.

His face was drawn as he stood up. He picked up the ring with hands that shook and put it into a tiny zipped pocket on the sleeve of his coat.

'This isn't the right place to talk,' he said.

'There's nothing more to say,' she replied sadly.

They drove home silently, but outside the Hartleys' house he turned to her and the expression in his eyes was full of hot intensity.

'This isn't the end. I refuse to let such a trivial issue come between us.'

She felt so much for him, but it gave him the power to hurt her.

'Goodbye, Daniel.' Her voice was a choked whisper.

She didn't look back as she walked down the path and pushed open the door of her parents' house. All she wanted was to get upstairs and give way to the wild grief that was tearing her apart.

But the lounge door flew open and Kevin shouted, 'Kay! Get in here! You'll never guess!'

'Later,' she called, trying to keep her voice steady.

She turned to run up the stairs, but her mother came out into the hall.

'Kayleigh! Our farm's up for sale. We need

you, love.'

She paused. She couldn't ignore her mother's summons.

She glanced at her reflection in the hall mirror. Her face was white and her violet eyes were dark and hurt, but otherwise she showed no trace of the turmoil inside her. She never did; her pretty face was the bane of her life. Would Daniel take her seriously if she were plain? But at least the features that nature had given her made it easy to hide her feelings from her family; nobody would know that her heart was broken.

The dining table was covered with estate agent's details and glossy bank leaflets. Bailey was frowning over a calculator, and crumpled pages of scrawled figures lay scattered around.

Her father looked up, and Kayleigh saw that his normally calm expression was alight. 'Here's our business whiz-kid! Come and see what you think of this, love.'

'Our farm's for sale!' Kevin announced. 'And we're going to buy it. Me and Charlene can afford a bit of the mortgage, but you've got to pay some as well.'

Mrs Hartley shushed him. 'Kayleigh might not want to, love – give her a chance.'

Kayleigh was filled with a sudden hot

excitement. Now she had a brilliant excuse to run away from this torment. On the wonderful salary the Americans were offering, she could pay for the mortgage on the farm with ease. And in New York she wouldn't give Daniel a thought.

'Oh, yes, I do!' she cried. 'In fact, I can afford the whole mortgage. I'm going to take that job in America and I'll buy the farm for you.'

Bill shook his head. 'Don't talk soft, our Kayleigh. As if me and your mum would let you do that. No, we don't need too much help from you, not if my figures are correct. Here – will you check them for me?'

The sum next to her name was astonishingly modest.

'But where will the rest come from?'

'Me and Sandra will be chipping in,' Bailey told her.

Sandra's eyes were dreamy with plans. 'We can take Tommy there in the holidays. I can just see him running around that garden. He'll love it!'

Bailey's eyes were bright. 'There are lovely big attics. I could convert them to a self-contained flat.'

'Not before you've put in my bathrooms,' Mrs Hartley said. 'And central heating as well, if you don't mind, love.'

'You can have whatever you want, as soon as you like,' Bailey said cheerfully. 'My other customers will just have to wait!'

Mavis beamed at him. 'Comes in handy, having your own builder!'

Kayleigh had checked the figures. 'They do add up,' she said. 'Even without getting top price for this house you can do it with ease, Dad. I never knew you had so much in the bank!'

He chuckled. 'We've been saving up. I always had it in mind that that farm would come on the market again one day.'

Kayleigh looked at the figures again. 'Let me pay more, though. I think Kevin's contribution is too high. The supermarket pays lousy wages, and he can't work more hours while he's still at school.'

Kevin shook his head. 'I'm paying my share, and I'm having my drum kit in the barn.'

Kayleigh looked round at her family's eager faces. 'You've got it all worked out, haven't you? Well, I'm in. And you can have what I made off the penthouse flat, too.'

'I'll bear that in mind,' her father said, 'but you'll be wanting another place yourself. Or you and Daniel, happen?'

Kayleigh stared hard at the paper in her hand. The figures blurred as she looked at them through the tears in her eyes. She swallowed hard.

'Daniel's history.'

She could feel her mother's sharp gaze on her face and her father looked troubled.

'What a shame! He were a bit posh, but I liked him.'

'He was the best you've ever brought home, Kayleigh,' Bailey put in. 'But there's plenty more fish in the sea.'

Mavis Hartley said nothing, but Kayleigh knew she was looking at her in the way that mothers do when they're finding out what you so want to hide! But that wise woman must have realised that she couldn't bear to talk about Daniel because she changed the subject back to the house.

'That's all settled then. We'll make an offer in the morning.'

'Are you going to offer less than the asking price?' Sandra asked. 'You might be able to save some money.'

Mr Hartley shook his head. 'I don't want to risk losing it. It's ours, that place is. Always has been.'

The rest of the family sat on, making excited plans, but Kayleigh hurt so much inside that it was difficult to join in the discussion – and to avoid her mother's eyes. Mavis was wise about people, and Kayleigh remembered how she had said that Daniel loved her that night he had come straight from the hospital in distress.

The tears she had been fighting threatened to overwhelm her.

'I'm going to bed,' she said abruptly.

Once she was free to cry, the tears wouldn't come, and she lay in bed staring at the ceiling in dry-eyed agony. She couldn't cry, but her throat throbbed and ached. She had weathered many storms in this room, but nothing had cut her so deeply as this.

A six a.m. her phone beeped, telling her that a text message had arrived. *Can't sleep. Miss you too much. Please see me?*

Kayleigh's phone had a useful item on the text menu. You pushed one button and the message flew back: *The answer is no.* She used it when he suggested breakfast together. She used it when he suggested morning coffee. She used it when he suggested lunch, and she used it again when he suggested afternoon tea. She was walking around the farmhouse on a viewing with her family by then.

'You're getting ever such a lot of texts,'

Charlene remarked.

'It's junk!' Kayleigh answered. 'Have you decided which bedroom you want?'

'This one!' Charlene said rapturously. 'You and me next to one another, Kevin in the back, Mum and Dad in the front, and Bailey and Sandra can make a flat out of the attics upstairs. It's perfect.'

Mavis's eyes were worried. 'It's too perfect. I don't think it's going to happen. The estate agent did say there are other offers. Somebody rich will get it.'

'We're rich!' Bill said stoutly. 'They'll accept our offer, you'll see. It's meant for us, this house. It's got our name on it.'

At that very moment his mobile phone rang, and the whole family fell silent, watching his expression anxiously as he took the call.

The delighted beam that crossed his face told them everything.

'It's ours!' he yelled.

For one blissful minute, Kayleigh was able to rejoice. But then her phone gave the beep that meant a text had arrived: *Please have dinner with a lonely man?*

She used that button again. *The answer is no.*

It was so hard to keep saying no and she was within an inch of giving in. She had taken Friday off to be with Daniel yesterday. The trip out to view the farmhouse had taken care of Saturday, but there was the rest of Saturday night to fill and the whole of Sunday, and they stretched before her like a desert. She loved him. She wanted him. And on Sunday morning she gave in.

His message said, *Just finished night shift – have breakfast with me?*

This time she replied, *Meet you for coffee @ Jazz.*

Back came a smiley face and a big row of kisses.

She didn't know if she was doing the right thing as she cycled towards the coffee bar, but she wanted to see him again so badly. And maybe now that he realised how important her eco-activism was to her, he would love her for herself instead of trying to turn her into the sort of person he thought would match her pretty face.

He was already at the coffee shop when she arrived, sitting in a big leather chair with the Sunday papers spread around him, and he looked so handsome that her knees melted beneath her.

He was on his mobile and didn't see her,

so she went to the counter and got herself a coffee and a wicked slice of coffee cake with cream and chocolate-covered beans on top. She was in the mood for celebrating. She was so happy to see him that she knew she had done the right thing in giving him another chance.

She sat down at his table just as he finished his call.

'Hi,' she said, feeling shy.

He gave her a merry grin. 'I've had a wonderful idea. How about I buy your badgers a tunnel?'

'In exchange for what, exactly?' she asked, hoping that she was wrong.

His face was still untroubled. 'Well, then you could forget that ridiculous campaign and we could be engaged again.'

She looked at the cake she had bought in such good spirits only a few moments ago. Now she thought she would never eat again.

'Daniel, don't you realise that I would simply move on to the next campaign?'

'Why? Why be so stubborn about it?'

She looked up at him sadly. 'Why can't you accept me as I am?'

'Because you're talking rubbish.'

'I do what I can to save the planet and I will continue to do so.'

There was a long pause this time, and Daniel's eyes darkened as he suddenly realised what was happening. 'Kayleigh, listen–'

She held up a hand. 'Forget it.'

'You have to let me try again,' he whispered, rubbing his hand over his eyes. 'I was working all night. I've had no sleep. Please…'

She felt so sad as she looked at him because she still loved him, but the answer had to be no. Firmly she shook her head.

'But I love you. I can't understand how we come to be arguing…'

The sight of his distress moved her and a huge part of her wanted to fling herself into his arms and say that she forgave him, that it didn't matter – but it did.

'You want a wife who looks like me but who behaves differently. Our relationship will never work if you keep trying to change me.'

'You were my dream come true,' he whispered. 'I've been lonely for so long without realising it. I was going to talk to you about having a family today, to see how you felt about it. I've never wanted anything so much in my life. A little girl with your eyes. Oh, Kayleigh…'

For a moment a vision of a laughing small

146

boy who looked like Daniel rose before her eyes to torment her. There was so much love in her to give to a child, or two, and to Daniel. But did he love her?

'How can I believe that you love me when you want to change the most important part of me? You love my face, Daniel, but not my soul.'

He stared at her with slow, sad realisation.

'I know I'm being critical,' he agreed. 'But your position seems extreme to me.'

'I'm moderate compared with some of my colleagues,' Kayleigh said, thinking of Tom and how dedicated he was.

'I just can't accept that your activities are suitable for such a beautiful and intelligent woman.'

'Then there's no point in us being engaged.'

She looked at his dear, familiar face. It was incredible to believe that she'd never even met him five and a half weeks ago. Now he was the centre of her life, and always would be, she felt, and yet the fact that he wanted to change her hurt her to her core.

He stood up when she did, looking at her sadly.

'This isn't the end. We can get over this, Kayleigh.'

She ran blindly from the coffee shop, sobs choking her and her eyes running with hot tears, and eventually found herself standing on a bridge over the canal. She leaned on the brick parapet and let the tears flow.

She wasn't alone for long.

'Are you all right, dear?' A lady dressed for church was looking at her with anxious eyes, and Kayleigh fought to speak over the steel claws that were gripping her voice and hurting her throat.

'I'm fine, thank you. I've had a row with my boyfriend, that's all.'

The woman gave her a kind smile. 'Oh, well, if you're meant for each other, he'll come round, don't you worry.'

'Thank you,' Kayleigh said, and was relieved when the woman left her, though she appreciated her kind intent.

Her mobile phone rang and she took it out of her pocket with a hand that shook. Daniel, of course. She could see the whole cycle starting up again. He would ring her and he would text her, and because she loved him so much, she would eventually give in, and he would be happy while he was looking at her pretty face, but as soon as she started campaigning, he would start trying to change her, and the whole row would begin again, over and over, for the rest of their lives.

She looked at his name flashing on the little display screen of her phone and in spite of everything she wanted to answer it.

Her heart beat faster as she stood on that bridge over the canal and looked out at the high brick buildings that lined the water. On the one hand lay Daniel and her love for him, and the turmoil he caused in her heart. On the other lay a straight clear path.

She took a deep breath. Her mind was made up.

'I want a man who'll love me for my soul,' she said aloud.

When her phone rang again, she impulsively tossed the little machine into the water. As it fell, it turned over and over, flashing in the sunlight, ringing all the while, before plopping into the brown waters of the canal.

As she drove home she felt numb, but calmer.

At home she avoided her mother, not asking herself why, and paced the bedroom floor impatiently.

When it was 9.00 a.m. in New York, and she knew that the recruitment agency there would have opened, she dialled their number with fingers that shook and when she spoke it was through lips as dry as the desert.

'Hello? It's Kayleigh Hartley here. Is your offer still open?'

Chapter Nine

New York, New York!

Kayleigh felt as though she already knew New York when she arrived, although she had never set foot in the U.S.A. before.

'It's because I've seen it in so many movies and TV shows,' she told one of her colleagues.

'Everybody loves New York,' her co-worker agreed.

But Kayleigh didn't. Daniel and all her friends and family had been right when they had tried to stop her going. It wasn't the right place for her.

Tom sent her an email saying construction was beginning on the badger tunnel, and she cried because she wasn't there. She was missing out on so much. She wanted to be part of renovating the family's farmhouse. She wanted to go fishing with her dad. She wanted to help Charlene with her physiotherapy. She wanted to take Tommy out in his pushchair. She wanted to go to the coffee bar with Tracy.

New York has a thousand and one places to meet and the Americans that she worked with were friendly, but kind as the new people were, they were no substitute for her old friends.

She yearned, too, to see a whole wide sky and not just a tiny slice of blue between the skyscrapers.

Still, she was where Daniel could no longer upset her, so she had achieved her aim, and she settled down to make the best of her new life. At least, she tried to, but she only seemed to get more miserable as the days and then weeks passed, until she had been in New York for three months and finally had to admit to herself that she hated it.

But Kayleigh had grit; she was no quitter. She would stay put and make the best of it.

The August weather was hot and humid, and she wondered if she would be happier when the cool crisp days of autumn came. But in the middle of September, while it was still hot, she got a phone call from home.

'Sandra?' Kayleigh questioned. 'Is Bailey all right? And Tommy?'

'Everything's fine at home,' her sister-in-law reassured her quickly. 'Little Tommy's well and Bailey's in the pink. Your dad made the others promise not to contact you, but I wasn't there at the time, so I haven't promised and I thought you'd want to know…'

'Know what?' Kayleigh asked anxiously. 'Is it Dad? What's wrong?'

'He's going into hospital at last to have the cartilage on that knee of his replaced. He'll be in for just a few days. I thought you might like to send him some flowers or a card or something.'

'Of course I will. Thanks for ringing me, Sandra.'

As Kayleigh put the phone down, she was gripped by a wave of love and longing to see her dad. It was so like him not to want to worry her.

Overnight her mind became clear, so that next morning, she went straight to her boss's office and asked for leave.

He shook his head. 'You haven't been with the company for long enough to be granted any vacation.'

'But my father's in hospital.'

'But you said it's a minor operation. Compassionate leave for something so small – it can't be done.'

'Can't I take unpaid leave?'

That head-shake again. 'We need you working on the cookie campaign.'

'Then I quit!' As soon as she said the words, she felt a surge of relief.

Her boss frowned. 'Hey, I don't think you've thought this through.'

She met his eyes squarely. 'I don't need to. My father's ill and no power on earth is going to keep me from him.'

He shrugged. 'We'll have to keep back some of your salary if you leave without completing your due period of notice.'

'You can keep the whole lot of it! I'm going back home, where I belong.' She realised how exhausting living a lie had been and felt a tremendous strain lifting from her shoulders.

Straight away she went to ring Sandra and tell her she was coming home, but she swore her sister-in-law to secrecy.

'I want to surprise Dad!'

She packed her bags and managed to get a seat on a flight that left New York on Friday morning, and finally stumbled out at Manchester Airport a crumpled, jet-lagged wreck, but so glad to be home.

Bailey was waiting for her in the arrivals hall and she hugged him as if she would never let him go. He gave her a huge grin.

'Missed us, did you? Dad's fine. Come on, I'll take you to the hospital.'

Manchester looked small after New York. The trees were still green, but she could see rain falling as they walked over the bridge to the car park. She could hear warm northern accents all around her and the air smelt deliciously familiar. She was so glad to be back in England that she could have fallen to the ground and kissed it. It was wonderful to sit next to Bailey in the same old builder's van and drive on the correct side of the road through areas she knew and loved.

'Tell me all about Dad's operation,' she demanded.

'He's fine, but don't ask me to get any more technical than that,' Bailey returned. 'How was your flight?'

'Tiring, but worth every second now that I'm back home.'

They talked about the weather in New York and England, and flight times and jet lag, until they arrived at the hospital.

'I don't know where we're going to park,' Kayleigh sighed, looking at the queue of traffic waiting to get into the car park. Frustration welled up in her. Having come so far, she wanted to see her father *now!*

However, to her surprise, Bailey turned

left and bypassed the queue. He not only had a pass into the staff car park, he also turned into a reserved spot, the one marked *Reserved for Mr Warner-Bond*. Only a racing bike occupied the space. It was chained to the wall, and tied to the seat was a large inflatable toad wearing a cycle helmet. Bailey chuckled.

'There's a new joke every time I come,' he said.

Kayleigh put the mystery of the bike aside to think about later. Right now she wanted to see her father.

Mr Hartley was in a general ward, sitting bolt upright wearing blue and white striped pyjamas. His cheeks were rosy. He looked fine.

The surprise in his round blue eyes was worth all her efforts.

'Kay! Well I never! Why aren't you at work?'

She didn't know whether to laugh or cry as he enveloped her in a hug.

'I've left, Dad. I didn't like it.'

He gazed lovingly into her eyes. 'I said all along that you'd be better off at home. How are you, chick? You look a bit peaky.'

'That's just after the flight. I'm fine. I want to know how you are.'

'All done and dusted!' he said. 'They're chucking me out tomorrow.'

'He's an old fraud,' Bailey agreed. 'I'd better get back to Sandra, Dad. Bye, Kayleigh – I'll bring your luggage round later.'

Kayleigh sat down next to her father. 'How are you really, Dad?'

He looked over her shoulder and his face brightened. 'Here's the man to tell you. I'm as fit as a butcher's dog, aren't I, Daniel?'

'Taking up space under false pretences,' agreed a familiar voice.

Kayleigh's breath caught as she looked up at him. He had haunted her dreams every night in America, and now here he was in reality.

He was surprised to see her. She saw all the shock of it on his face. And his eyes blazed with a force that usually lay hidden under his calm exterior.

Her senses responded passionately to the man, but first, he could tell her what she so needed to know.

'Is Dad honestly all right?' she asked.

He nodded, and Kayleigh felt a tear of relief trickle down her cheek. At once Daniel's arms went around her, and at last she felt she was truly home. His strong arms were wrapped around her, his chest was warm, and she felt safe leaning against him. The feel and the smell of him took her back to all those weeks ago when he'd first kissed her, and she had dreamed of him so often since that it was incredible to be in his arms.

He held her with tight, tight arms until the first rush of tears was over and she lifted her head and looked at him. She could feel his heart thudding, and was glad that he was as moved as she was. His eyes were alight with joy and fervour as he examined her face.

A large white linen handkerchief appeared in his hands and she took it gratefully and mopped at her eyes until she was back in control.

'I'm sorry.'

'You were worried – it's only natural,' Daniel said, as he had said to her once before. He released her then, but his loving gaze never left her.

'Have you stopped crying, you daft sausage?' Bill Hartley said.

'If you're going to insult me,' Kayleigh said, taking the American fishing magazines she had brought him out of her bag and tipping them on to the bed, 'I won't give you anything to read.'

Bill reached for them eagerly, and as his attention was caught at once by the cover of one, his nose vanished into its pages.

Kayleigh looked at Daniel. 'He's forgotten I'm here,' she said, meeting his eyes and smiling.

His eyes were brilliant as they smiled back, yet all his stiffness and formality had returned, and was that unease lurking in his expression?

'What's wrong?' she asked, and glanced at her father. 'What aren't you telling me?'

'He's fine,' he assured her quickly. 'But there is another matter.'

He had changed, she was sure of it. He was thinner and looked fitter, but it wasn't just that. He looked younger, yet more mature at the same time; softer, yet more confident. She loved the new Daniel even more than the old one. She wanted to reach out and touch him, take his hand and be close to him, but when she reached out for his hand he drew away.

'Kayleigh, you said you were never coming back...'

Fear clutched at her heart because suddenly he wouldn't meet her eyes. He looked away from her, and when she followed the direction of his gaze, she saw a familiar figure, frumpy despite the brightness of her magenta and orange tweed, marching down the ward.

'Daniel! I've been waiting for you in the car park for absolutely ages! We need to alert security, because your space has been vandalised again. I suppose it's medical students trying to be funny, but I can't think why they're targeting you with those stupid frogs. And, rather more seriously, there was a disreputable white van parked in your space when I arrived. Really, people have no respect these days. I took the registration number so that we can report him.'

'Sorry, Fiona,' Daniel said. 'I forgot to tell you that I've loaned my parking permit to Kayleigh's brother.'

Muddy brown eyes met Kayleigh's, and for a moment Fiona looked aghast to see her, but then her eyes blazed with triumph and she put her left hand on Daniel's arm in an intimate gesture.

'Good, then we can go straight to Nanton. You know how lucky we were to get an appointment with the vicar. He wouldn't have squeezed us in at all if he and Mummy weren't such good pals.'

Fiona's words were apparently addressed to Daniel, but Kayleigh read the message in them as clear as a bell, and her gaze flew to the woman's hand. A large Victorian engagement ring made of many different stones sparkled and gleamed on the third finger.

Shocked, she turned to stare at Daniel.

'I'll have to leave now,' he said steadily. 'I'm glad to see your father in such good health.'

Stunned, Kayleigh watched Fiona take his hand and tow him firmly down the ward and out of sight. A lump like a stone seemed to rise up in her throat and choke her. She was glad when a bell rang and people began stirring and collecting their belongings.

'Dad, visiting time's over.'

He looked up from his fishing magazine, his mind still so engaged by the fabulous photographs that he didn't notice her stricken expression.

'Give us a kiss then, chick,' he said absently. 'It's nice to have you back.'

Kayleigh walked out of the hospital and wandered towards the main road to catch a bus. The September day was grey and a light but wetting drizzle fell.

There was no longer any comfort in the idea that she was going home. She rested her forehead against the cold, vibrating glass of the bus window and stared blindly at the rain rolling down the flat surface. She felt worse now than she had while she was exiled in

America and she realised that underneath her previous misery had always been the comforting thought that she could come home any time, and the arrogant certainty that Daniel would be glad to see her.

Well, now she was home, and he was engaged to another woman. Yet he had been pleased to see her. His eyes had blazed with love and his heart had raced while he held her, so how could he possibly be promised to Fiona, of all people? The one woman he'd said he would never marry! And only a few months after he'd asked Kayleigh to marry him.

It was an effort to paste a smile on her face as she walked up the familiar path to her house.

'Anybody home?' she called as she opened the door.

Her mother was in the kitchen packing cookery books into a crate but she spun round in amazement at the sound of her voice.

'Well, I never! Look who's here! Have you been to see your dad?'

Kayleigh hugged and kissed her. 'Bailey took me to the hospital straight from the airport. He had a staff parking pass and everything.'

'Daniel's been lovely,' Mavis said, her gaze raking Kayleigh's face. 'He couldn't do enough for your dad.'

'Was that his bike parked in the space? There was no sign of his car.'

'He's just taken it up. That'll be your influence, perhaps.'

Kayleigh looked away. There was no way she could discuss Daniel just now. She looked at the chaos of packing that littered the house and tried to speak cheerfully.

'It's a pity Dad couldn't go straight to the new place.'

'It'll be another few weeks yet, love. We might not be moved in before you have to go back to America, what with the building work and all.'

'Ah,' Kayleigh said. 'Mum, there's something I have to tell you…'

Her mother was delighted when she heard she was home for good.

'What a blessing – you can help us sell this house. Bailey will do the work, of course, but he'd be the first to admit he's useless with colours, so I want you to choose the new décor. It seems you don't get the best price for a place if you don't gussie it up these days.'

'I'd love to help,' Kayleigh said. 'I'll be

glad to have something to do – besides job hunting, of course. I've never had to look for a job before!'

'Well, now's your chance to take a bit of time and see what's out there. Unless you're thinking about going back to your old place, that is?'

Kayleigh shook her head. 'Nick Corkish was no replacement for Joan.'

'Joan was very good to you, that's a fact. Don't worry, chick. The right job is out there. It's wonderful how things come good.'

'You always say that,' Kayleigh teased.

'And I'm always right,' her mother retorted. 'If you have faith and take the long view, things always work out for the best.'

Kayleigh found it hard to believe that as the next miserable week crawled by. She caught up with the latest on the badger tunnel and threw herself into cleaning, packing and renovating the old house, but there was still so much time to think.

She was delighted when Tracy rang on Monday and suggested coffee at lunch-time.

'You won't believe how much I missed this place when I was in New York,' she told her friend. 'Nowhere else plays my favourite rock and roll.'

Tracy looked at her critically.

'You look rough, if you don't mind my saying so. What's wrong?'

'Daniel's engaged to someone else,' Kayleigh told her, slowly stirring the froth on her coffee.

'No! I can't believe it! You've only been away – what, a couple of months?'

'Three. And I did tell him I was never coming back. I told him it was over.'

'Then he's stupid. How could he have believed you?'

'I meant it,' Kayleigh admitted quietly.

'Who's he engaged to?'

'Fiona.'

'What, the horsy bore you told me about?'

'He's known her since they were little.'

Tracy snorted. 'I bet she made a swift move while he was miserable. He *was* miserable when you left him, wasn't he?'

'You think? He got over it fast enough.'

'Oh, no, he didn't. I bet it's only because he was so devastated that Fiona got through his defences. I bet he was bowled over to see you again. Did he say anything?'

'Not a word,' Kayleigh said, but she couldn't help remembering the fast beat of his heart.

'Well,' Tracy said, 'you should never have left in the first place, but you wouldn't listen when we all told you, would you? Now you'll just have to get him back.'

'Fiona will never let him go. She's always wanted him.' Kayleigh sighed. 'Anyway, it's no business of mine. Let's forget it…'

'Excuse me,' a voice said behind them. A middle-aged lady in a pink fleece stood smiling at them. 'I don't know if you remember me'

'Of course I do!' Kayleigh said. 'Tracy, this is Pauline, the lady who runs the animal sanctuary.'

'Hi,' Tracy said, smiling warmly. 'Kayleigh's told me about your place. I think you do great work. I'll put one of your new collecting boxes in my salon, if you like.'

The woman hesitated and pushed back a few wisps of blonde hair.

'I don't want to cause any trouble or anything, but nothing's arrived: no collecting boxes, no leaflets, no posters, nothing.'

Kayleigh was astonished. 'But I signed off on it all months ago, before I went to the States. Did you contact Vale's to ask them about it?'

'Well, yes, but you know, now that Joan's not there any more, and with you leaving as well … they didn't seem to want to talk to me.'

'Well, they'll talk to me,' Kayleigh said grimly, and pulled out her phone.

A frustrating fifteen minutes later she broke the connection and stared at Pauline. Tracy had had to leave, to get back to her salon.

'I'm sorry I took so long.' She drummed her fingers on the tabletop. 'Nick Corkish finally agreed that I can have the artwork, though he was less than willing about it. I'll go now and collect it before he changes his mind. We'll have to find the money to get the items made, I'm afraid, but at least you won't have to pay for the design work.'

'Not everyone is as generous as Joan,' Pauline commented. 'I wish there was more like her, and you, of course. Thanks for your help, love.'

'It's no trouble,' Kayleigh said, getting to her feet. 'In fact, a good fight was exactly what I needed!'

Nick handed over the fundraising artwork with no more arguments. In fact, there was an almost apologetic expression in his eyes.

'Times are hard. We've had to cut back on our charity work, but I don't like doing it,' he explained.

'Joan used to say that if you waited until you felt you could afford to give to charity, that moment would never arrive,' Kayleigh retorted, but she could tell he didn't get it. He was thinking along different lines.

'Would you consider coming back?' he asked. 'We'd raise your salary. The new chap's not as good as you were. In fact, we've lost several of your accounts. People want you, Kayleigh. They value your work, and so do we.'

The praise was sweet, but all her instincts were against it.

'Thank you, but my mind's made up.'

Nick sighed, and then a predatory look sprang into his eyes.

'Well, if I'm not to be your boss again, how about dinner one evening? You always said you wouldn't date a colleague, but there's nothing stopping us now.'

She gave him one of her best glares. 'Apart from the fact that I'd rather stick hot needles in my eyes!'

Men! She was fuming as she walked along the pavement clutching her big portfolio, but Nick's reaction had proved that she was right not to go back to her old job. It had turned into a company where she wouldn't be happy. Still, she urgently needed a job. She had better buy a paper and check the situations vacant on the tram home.

However, the front page story took her mind away from job hunting: *Latest on Bicycle Factory Protest* announced the headlines.

The number of protesters camped outside Bond's Cycle Factory swelled again today. Our reporter asked factory manager Hugo Morton (34) if it was true that sales have fallen dramatically because furious customers are refusing to buy mountain bikes from a company that destroys trees.

'It's just a load of stupid rumours put about by trouble-makers,' fumed Hugo. 'Those trees were damaging the factory and had to be cut down. Only freaks and extremists would make a fuss.'

Eco-Warrior "Mole Man" (22) refuted this hotly.

'That's just so, like, not true,' he told our reporter. 'People totally care about trees and if they don't buy any more bikes then the company won't need a new factory and the planet can breathe easy. It's a no-brainer, dude.'

The troubled mountain bike company refused to admit that sales have plummeted to zero, but leading Manchester bicycle retailers confirmed today that their customers are boycotting Bond's Bikes in favour of greener companies.

Kayleigh read the story twice, and then she put it aside with a sigh. It was nothing to do with her.

Or so she believed until the next day when the telephone rang at home. It was for her.

'Kayleigh, it's Peter Warner-Bond. Daniel told me you're home. I hope you don't mind my ringing? I don't know how busy you might be, but I was wondering if you would consider helping us out. I'm afraid my company is in need of your expertise to rescue us from a public relations disaster.'

Kayleigh's mind raced. Blimey, she was being asked to work as a consultant. A picture of herself running her own independent agency sprang into her mind. It was a huge step, but it was logical. She could do it, she knew she could. All she needed was the confidence to strike out on her own.

The voice on the phone said, 'Of course, I'll understand if you would rather not. I'm particularly conscious that if we had taken your advice in the first place, the company would not now be suffering the way it is.'

'Of course I'll help you. When would you like to meet?'

'Now!' Peter said with evident relief. 'A young lady constructed a tree-house in the oak tree by the gate last night and she says she's going to live there. We're quite at a loss as to how to handle the situation.'

Kayleigh arranged to meet him at his office so that she could see the scale of the protest for herself. Then, remembering her little brother was off school with a cold, she ran upstairs and knocked on his door.

'Kevin, I need a letterhead for my new business. Are you well enough to use your computer?'

'Course I am!' Kevin snuffled. 'Bet I can design you a logo as well in the time it takes you to get ready!'

Kayleigh got ready for her meeting with unusual care, choosing a designer suit that she had bought in New York. She wanted to look her most professional when she handed over her first independent estimate.

Peter accepted it without a blink.

'If I don't succeed, you don't have to pay me,' she told him.

'The company's facing bankruptcy and two hundred people could lose their jobs,' Peter replied. 'If you're able to rescue us, I shall double your fee. I bitterly regret not speaking to that "Mole Man" lad as you suggested in the first place.'

'Have you had any contact with him?'

'No. Hugo was against the idea. He was convinced it was a single eccentric. And a couple of weeks ago Hugo succeeded in obtaining a court injunction. He thought that if the young man was forbidden to come near the factory, the fuss would die down. But it had the opposite effect. It was like pouring oil on a bonfire. There are hundreds of people outside today – well, you saw them.'

'I did,' Kayleigh said. 'And I looked at Mole Man's website this morning. Have you read it?'

'Website? Well, no. I'm not very *au fait* with computers, I'm afraid.'

Kayleigh was firm. 'You need to read it. You need to understand the issue from the protesters' point of view. Where can we find a computer that's connected to the Internet?'

Peter led her into the main office, where people were hanging around in knots, whispering and looking worried. The phone never stopped ringing, but nobody picked it up – the calls were left to go straight to voicemail. Kayleigh shook her head. Refusing to speak to people was no way to handle a tricky situation, but she would take it one step at a time.

Peter sat down in front of the nearest

computer and looked at it warily.

In a few clicks Kayleigh had Mole Man's website displayed on the screen for him. It was bright, colourful, passionate and heartfelt, and within a few seconds Peter was reading with fierce concentration. He read every page on the site, looked at the photographs of the fallen trees, and then read the pages of email messages in support of the campaign.

When he had finished he pushed his chair back and looked at her with stunned misery in his eyes. 'Bond's Cycles is finished. After reading that, I feel as if *I* ought to join the campaign against my own company. There is no defence. We have behaved dreadfully.'

He checked the date the site had been created and sighed.

'A few days after I spoke with you. If I had met him then as you advised, if I had understood how bad the facts could look, how strongly he felt, we might have been able to reach a compromise, but now...'

'Don't give up,' Kayleigh advised. 'I have a few ideas. But next, I need to meet with your operations director and anyone else who's involved.'

'Hugo has called an emergency meeting of the board for three o'clock tomorrow.

Would you find it helpful to attend?'

'Perfect, especially if you need their approval before putting my campaign into action. It'll save us lots of time. Until then, do you have an office I can work in?'

'Take mine. Ask for anything you want, anything at all.'

Kayleigh worked hard and well through the rest of the day and all the next morning. Peter insisted on taking her for lunch in the factory canteen, which was full of unhappy, idle factory hands.

'In another few days we'll have to start laying off staff,' he explained grimly. 'I'll delay it for as long as possible, of course. I feel bitterly that I have let everyone down.'

'Don't despair until you've heard my plan,' she said. 'My ideas are coming together nicely. This situation could be over in less than a week.'

Peter smiled at her with the blue eyes that made him look so like Daniel.

'Your confidence is heartening. Do you know, I find I have absolute faith in you.' He paused. 'Given the circumstances, it's very good of you to concern yourself with our troubles in this manner.'

'Circumstances?' she queried, wondering

how much he knew.

'Daniel once told me that he intended to marry you.'

'But he didn't love me,' she said sadly.

He seemed surprised. 'What makes you think that?'

'He liked my face, but not what's in my heart. When he learned more about my beliefs and passions, he wanted me to be different.'

'"Love is not love which alters when it alteration finds",' Peter murmured softly.

'"True love encompasses every bit of you and doesn't change",' she returned.

'Shakespeare was very wise about love and relationships.'

'You can't have a healthy relationship with anybody who won't let you be yourself,' she agreed.

'And Daniel thought he would love you only if you gave up what you believe in and behaved in a manner that suited him?' Peter asked incredulously.

'Yes.'

He stared blindly into the distance for a long, long moment, then he seemed to shake himself and said, 'Tea. Let me get you a cup of tea.'

When he came back with the tea, he had

clearly put personal feelings to one side and wanted to talk about the campaign. Kayleigh seized the chance to explain her own connection with environmental activism, but Peter took the news calmly.

'I trust your professionalism. If your friendship with Mole Man makes it easier to resolve this situation, then it could be a very good thing. I'm deeply thankful for your help and expertise.'

'Well, I should thank you as well. I needed the opportunity to go it alone. It's going to work out for everyone.'

Peter's sigh came up from the tips of his toes.

'I only hope we can convince the board of that.'

Chapter Ten

Boardroom Battle

By three o'clock Kayleigh had all her ideas in place and a whole campaign mapped out. Peter took her through to the boardroom and sat next to her at the polished oval table.

First to arrive were Fiona and Ruth, who sat together. Next came Hugo, the operations manager, in company with another man who had darting eyes and a shifty expression. Hugo seated his visitor, then flung himself into a chair next to him and began chatting to his sister as if he hadn't a care in the world.

Next came the finance director, the sales manager and the company lawyer, all in dark suits, then a secretary to take the minutes, and finally, to Kayleigh's surprise, Daniel. He sat down next to Fiona, who instantly kissed his cheek and put a possessive hand on his arm.

Ruth looked at her son with more warmth

in her amber eyes than Kayleigh had ever seen her display before. 'Oh, Daniel, I'm so glad you could be here.'

He smiled at his mother, but there was no real happiness in his eyes.

'Dad's always telling me I should take more interest in the business,' he explained.

'You've got your own career to think about,' Fiona snapped. 'You told me you had a paper to finish for your conference.'

Daniel gently moved his arm out of her grasp. 'Later,' he said.

He looked across the table and met Kayleigh's eyes. He was different. He had always been a kind man, but now the warmth was more visible under the professional calm.

Peter rose and cleared his throat. 'I think we're all here. This extraordinary meeting of the board has been called in order to deal with the difficult situation in which we currently find ourselves. I hope we can find a way to deal with the challenge.'

Hugo slapped the table, narrowed his brown eyes and gestured to the man he had brought with him. 'This is Frederick. He runs a security company. He knows how to deal with these people. I want you to authorise me to hire his firm. He'll provide

178

experienced men to chuck out these protesting yobs and then we can all get down to business.'

Peter stirred uneasily, but he inclined his head towards Frederick. 'Would you care to outline your plan for the benefit of the board?'

Frederick spoke clearly, but his gaze slid around the room and he looked at no one directly.

'You've got to be firm. You can't give them an inch. My men will soon clear the area and they won't stand no nonsense. If you act weak, scum like what's outside will take advantage of you. I'll get rid of them for you.'

Peter looked steadily at the man. 'At least ninety per cent of the protestors are on the public highway. How would you propose approaching them?'

Frederick looked at Peter for a second and winked.

'Well, maybe a hosepipe will accidentally point the wrong way and soak 'em. If that doesn't work, I know where I can borrow a muck spreader, and if the driver has a little accident, well, we won't waste any sleep over it, will we? You can leave it to me. I know a hundred tricks.'

Peter regarded the man with grave disfavour, then looked steadily at Hugo. 'And you endorse this plan of action?'

Hugo nodded vigorously. 'We need to blow those yobs out of the water.'

'Ruth?' Peter looked at his wife, who in turn looked hard at the table.

'You know I try to support Hugo,' she said.

Peter glared at her. 'There are women among the protestors,' he began, then bit off his words and visibly controlled himself.

He turned to the other directors. 'Any other comments?'

Chairs around the table shifted and paper rustled, but nobody spoke.

'We'll come back to your proposal, Hugo, but first, I'd like you to hear what Miss Hartley has to say.'

Hugo lounged back in his chair. 'Oh, little Miss Barbie talks, does she?' he sneered. 'I thought you'd brought her along to sit on top of the Christmas tree.'

'Hugo!' Peter and Daniel bellowed simultaneously.

'Kindly do my guest the courtesy of listening to her proposal with the same attention and consideration we gave your guest,' Peter said icily.

Hugo smirked. His whole air was untroubled and free from self-doubt.

'Mine's the only sensible course of action, but just as you like.'

Kayleigh got to her feet. She felt nervous with Daniel watching her, he was a distraction and she needed to keep her mind on the job.

She took a deep breath and began. 'It seems to me, Mr Morton, that you're viewing the protestors outside as enemies to be defeated.' Her mouth was dry. She stopped and cleared her throat.

Hugo was still grinning, but he was looking at her directly now and there was nothing jolly in his mean brown eyes.

'Well, hello-o – Barbie! There are a hundred unwashed agitators outside, ruining our business. You want me to be friends with them?'

Kayleigh nodded. 'That's exactly what I want–'

Hugo rocked forward on his chair and slammed his fist on the table. 'Oh, please! Get this bimbo out of here!'

Peter turned to the secretary. 'You may minute Hugo's objection, but kindly note that in my capacity as chairman I have instructed Miss Hartley to continue.'

Hugo got out his mobile phone and began tapping out a text message.

Ruth looked shocked by his rudeness. 'Hugo, can't your call wait?'

He gave her a nasty grin. 'Peter might have time to waste, but I don't.'

Peter's lips drew into a thin line, but he turned calmly to Kayleigh. 'Please carry on.'

She smiled at him to indicate that Hugo didn't worry her at all, and then looked at the people around the board table.

'In my opinion you're talking about the wrong issue. Your problem as a company is not the protestors outside the gate, it's the fact that your customers are boycotting your product.'

The finance director sat up and gazed at her with sharp interest.

'I'm sure Frederick is very efficient,' she continued, 'and he may well be able to encourage the protestors to move away from this building, but how would you stop them from campaigning in cyberspace? News of this dispute has reached all of your customers via the Internet. The boycott is worldwide, is it not?'

Now the sales manager was listening intently and nodded. 'The Germans cancelled an order this morning,' she said.

Hugo's phone beeped and he began another text message. Kayleigh was pleased to see Ruth glare at him. *He* might not be listening, but she knew the rest of the room was.

'This is a fight you cannot win,' she said firmly. 'Therefore, you must take the opposite tack. Bond's Cycles has made a mistake. You damaged the environment and your customers care about the environment. I want you to tell the protestors that you're sorry. You can't put the mature trees back, but you *can* plant new ones; you can sponsor a piece of rainforest, contribute to the carbon dioxide replacement fund – there's a lot to choose from. I have a detailed plan of action which I can show you for consideration later, if you decide to take my advice.'

Professional or not, she couldn't resist looking at Daniel to see what his response was. He looked back at her with bright eyes.

Fiona was watching him, a suspicious crease between her eyebrows. 'What's the matter, Daniel? You look as if somebody's dropped a bag of cement on your head.'

He ignored her. All his attention was on Kayleigh. He spoke slowly, as if he was thinking aloud. 'Hugo's not listening to you. He hasn't considered your ideas. He took one look at your blonde prettiness and switched off. Is that how I treated you?'

She bit her lip and nodded. 'Sometimes.'

Oblivious to the curious stares of the others, Daniel spoke softly as if they were alone together. 'Hugo has just made the biggest mistake of his professional career. It may end up costing him his position. But he's a lucky, lucky man. I made the same mistake, and it's going to cost me the rest of my life.'

'Daniel, what's going on?' Fiona was sharp, worried. 'What are you talking about? You haven't made any mistakes!'

His gaze never left Kayleigh's face. 'Oh, yes, I have,' he murmured, and Kayleigh felt tears sting her eyes.

Hugo sprang to his feet and let out a bear-like growl. 'Who do you think you are to say I could lose my job? I vote more stock than you do! And Ruth supports me.'

Ruth suddenly spoke up. 'I will vote with my husband. I support Peter.'

'Oh, my dear,' Peter said, and moved towards her. She rose and they embraced, her face soft and sad with emotion.

'I've been such a fool. I thought I was helping Hugo by always favouring him. I was trying to make up for the way his father treated him, but I see now that I was wrong.'

Peter kissed her tenderly. 'You acted from the best of intentions.'

'Ruth!' Hugo roared furiously and banged on the table again. 'You promised to vote for me! What's got into everyone? Are you out of your minds? This is a board meeting, not a soap opera.'

But Peter and Ruth were engrossed in their reconciliation.

Kayleigh looked at the man she loved and wished she could go to him, while Daniel looked back at her with eyes full of anguish, but they were trapped by the situation.

Fiona was staring angrily at Daniel. She gripped his arm. When he still didn't look at her, she shook it. 'How can you be so ungrateful? If it wasn't for Hugo running the factory you wouldn't have been free to study medicine. I thought you promised to support him?'

Daniel had to shake his head and run a hand over his face before he could collect himself sufficiently to answer.

'I'm sure your brother has always acted with good intentions, Fiona, but I'm convinced that it's in the best interests of the company to follow Kayleigh's advice.'

Fiona's eyes screwed up furiously and she

rounded on Kayleigh. 'You troublemaker!'

'Order! Order!' The finance director pounded on the polished table.

Peter recovered himself and smiled at his wife. 'My dear, we'll talk later. Will you excuse me if I return to business?'

Ruth's eyes glimmered with happiness. 'Of course, darling.'

As they returned to their seats, Fiona's brown eyes scrunched up with temper. 'Daniel, what's got into you? You have to see sense!'

His eyes were infinitely sad. 'I have, but it's too late.'

'Daniel, listen to me–'

'Order!' said the finance director once more, and everyone subsided except Hugo.

'If you think I'm going to go out there and hug trees, you've got another think coming! I want immediate authority to employ Frederick and his men to take care of this problem the sensible way.'

Peter looked around the room. 'Would anyone care to second that proposal?'

The question was met with total, unbroken silence.

Hugo looked at the faces around the gleaming board table with slow-witted puzzlement, then focused on Ruth. 'Ruth?'

She shook her head. 'No, Hugo. It's time I stopped favouring you.'

Hugo turned his wrath on his sister. 'What do you have to say for yourself? How can you vote against your own brother?'

Kayleigh felt sorry for the woman. Fiona's dilemma was clear on her face as she looked at her brother and then at her fiancé.

'It's me or Daniel,' Hugo snarled.

Fiona bowed her head and looked at her hands twisting in her lap.

Hugo's gaze rested on her for a long moment. 'Ungrateful brat!'

He looked around the room and laughed bitterly. 'What about the rest of you? Are you all against me?'

'This is a business decision,' the finance director said calmly. 'Please don't take it personally.'

'How else *can* I take it? I either run the place or I don't! A factory needs a strong man in charge. I can't be doing with this touchy-feely stuff. Nothing ever gets decided.'

'Well, Hugo, perhaps a bit more of the "touchy-feely stuff", as you call it, would have prevented the situation from deteriorating,' the sales manager put in. 'I feel now that I made a mistake in not voting with

Peter to talk with the protestors in the first instance. You must admit that your handling of the situation so far has not helped matters. In fact, it has escalated into a nightmare. The company is facing ruin.'

Hugo stared at the woman, red mottled patches showing in his cheeks.

'How dare you stab me in the back, you treacherous cat? Have you forgotten who gave you your job in the first place?'

'I'm only interested in what is best for the company.'

Hugo stared around the room, breathing heavily. 'Well, I'm through! I quit! You try it the Barbie way, and when it all goes horribly wrong you can come crawling back to me. If I'm not too busy I might, I just might, come and help you out.'

He strode out of the room and slammed the door behind him.

Frederick followed, remarking loudly as he went, 'Waste of an afternoon.'

The secretary looked at Peter, a worried crease between her eyes. 'How should I minute all that?'

He looked sad for a minute and then smiled. 'Please record Mr Hugo Morton's objections, his vote against the board's decision, and his verbal resignation.' He lifted his head and gazed around the room. 'All those in favour of Kayleigh's proposal?'

The 'Aye' was unanimous, and he smiled at Kayleigh. 'My dear, we are in your hands. What's the next step?'

But Kayleigh was having trouble concentrating on formulating her reply. She could hear Fiona nagging Daniel.

'Come home with me and finish your paper for the conference. You know you hate business. What on earth do you want to get involved with all this for?'

'Perhaps I want to support my father through a difficult situation,' he pointed out reasonably, and Peter smiled at him with surprised eyes.

'I thought you didn't care about the factory.'

Daniel shrugged. 'You've never needed me before. I don't care about the day-to-day running of the business, it's true, but I care about you, and if there's trouble, then I want to be here for you.'

Fiona tugged at Daniel's arm. 'I've packed you a case. You can't miss your American conference.'

'On the contrary, I can easily miss the conference.'

'But you'll never make professor if you

don't give that paper,' Fiona cried despairingly.

'I wouldn't have a career at all if my father and the factory hadn't supported me. This is the first time I've ever been in a position to return that support. It means more to me than a job title ever could.'

Peter was visibly moved. 'Daniel, my boy…'

Even now the two men were standing at least a foot apart in the best British tradition, but Daniel smiled at his father with a world of love in his eyes. 'I haven't always appreciated your efforts as much as I might have, but then, I've been a fool in many ways. You must let me make good my stupidity.'

Peter stepped forward and touched his son on the shoulder. The fleeting gesture said more than words ever could. 'I owe you an apology of my own. I was wrong to try to force you into the factory. You're a fine man and a brilliant doctor. That's enough to make any father proud.'

'Dad…' Daniel began, and then emotion welled up in him and his next words came so softly that only those nearest to him could hear. 'All my life I've wished that I could please you.'

Peter shook his head. 'I was wrong to want you to be different. Kayleigh taught me that love means accepting people for who they are, not who you wish they were.'

Daniel looked at Kayleigh, his eyes very soft. 'I realise that now.'

His father's eyes were sad and wise. 'You learned your attitude from me. I'm sorry for that, as for much else. I want you to go to your conference. I appreciate your support, but with Kayleigh's help, this crisis will soon be over.'

Daniel's eyes were dark. 'I know. I have absolute faith in her.'

Kayleigh couldn't stop staring at him. At last he respected her, yet she was miserable. She wanted him back, and she couldn't have him.

Peter cleared his throat and became the businessman. 'Go finish your paper!' he commanded, waving Daniel and Fiona out of the room. Then he turned to Kayleigh. 'What's our next action?'

She looked at her watch. It was nearly five o'clock.

'Could you send out a message asking your staff to join you for a meeting first thing in the morning? Make it clear that we have a recovery plan and that we'll be asking for their help in seeing it through.'

The finance director shrugged. 'If Peter says come to a meeting, the staff will turn up. You don't have to explain yourself.'

Kayleigh chose her words carefully because she didn't want to antagonise the man. 'The situation is so serious that people could think you're about to announce redundancies.'

He looked at her face for a moment, examining her with the cool clever eyes of a money man, and then he nodded. 'I see your point. Our staff has no idea what happened today, and without you, we *would,* in sober fact, have been announcing redundancies tomorrow.'

The secretary glanced at Peter and he nodded. 'Please take Kayleigh's instructions.'

The woman rushed off to announce the meeting and Peter turned to Kayleigh. 'What's next?'

She grinned and pushed up her sleeves. 'A lot! Let's go! Does anyone know the weather forecast for tomorrow?'

Chapter Eleven

A Triumph

Despite the pouring rain and the early hour, when Kayleigh arrived at the cycle works the next morning she saw a crowd of around five hundred people flocking around the factory gates. Although she knew many of them, she suddenly realised how intimidating they looked as a group. She didn't want to be recognised yet, so she hunched deeper behind her dark glasses and sun visor, and drove slowly through the placard-waving, slogan-chanting protestors, praying that her plan would work.

As she pulled into a visitors' parking space, she spotted Daniel's sleek saloon and her heart kicked. She sat quietly for a moment, gathering her composure before stepping out into the rain.

She was wind-blown and damp by the time she reached the sanctuary of the building, but at least her demeanour was calm as she greeted Daniel, even though he looked devastating in jeans and a charcoal-grey fleece. His greeting was equally restrained, but his eyes burned when he looked at her.

Peter stepped forward and kissed Kayleigh on the cheek. 'I'm very glad to see you, my dear, but I'm worried. None of the promotional items has arrived. Should we phone the suppliers?'

Kayleigh glanced at her watch. 'The goods aren't promised until eight o'clock and Mr Arshif has never let me down. It might be better to get on with the staff meeting.'

'Just as you wish.' Peter glanced at her. 'Are you sure you want to address the meeting yourself? Despite the reassurances you so sensibly suggested we offer, the staff are somewhat agitated.'

'I'll be fine so long as you introduce me the way we agreed.'

Daniel looked at Kayleigh and then spoke to his father. 'I'm sure Kayleigh will do a far better job of winning over the staff than you or I ever could.'

Kayleigh felt warmed to her heart by his compliment.

Peter smiled at her. 'I think Daniel may be right. We'll soon find out. All the staff are ready and waiting.'

Kayleigh did feel apprehensive as she

followed Peter and Daniel into the large staff canteen where the two hundred factory workers were gathered. It was incredibly nerve-wracking standing at the head of the room listening to Peter introducing her. She told herself that all she was going to do was talk to a few reasonable people, but she felt as if she was going into an arena to fight lions.

Her heart didn't stop bumping until she had explained her point of view and could see from the nodding heads all around her that, by and large, the staff were in sympathy with her plan.

One worker spoke for them all. 'I hated walking through those lines this morning. I mean, you have to think about keeping your job, but I haven't liked being the bad guy. I'd be happy to say the company's sorry for cutting down those trees. I think we ought to be.'

Kayleigh turned to the presentation she was projecting from her laptop and showed the assembled staff a giant blow-up of a postcard. On the front was a powerful image of a man on a mountain bike tearing through a beautiful pine forest.

'You'll recognise this photograph from the latest brochure,' she said.

'Aye, it's Bobby, is that!' someone called, and a stir ran around the canteen as people turned to look at a blushing young man.

'It's a great picture,' Kayleigh said. 'We thought it would be a good image for the protestors to take away with them. I hope several thousand postcards will arrive very, very shortly and what I'd like you all to do is to go out and distribute them to the protestors outside.'

This didn't go down so well. Jaws dropped, and protests rang around the room:

'I wouldn't know what to say!'

'Management caused this row! Let them put it right.'

'I don't want to get involved.'

'Who's going to care if I say I'm sorry? I'm just an ordinary bloke.'

'Have you noticed the weather? Them postcards will be washed away in two minutes!'

Although Kayleigh listened to each objection calmly, Daniel looked at the grumbling staff and jumped to his feet, and she felt her heart pick up speed as he walked towards her. His eyes were bright, worried for her.

'I know I promised not to interfere, but…'

She smiled at him. 'Your dad's still sitting tight. He's got faith in me.'

Conceding the point, he stepped back, but he didn't move away, instead staying close to her. She knew he was ready to leap to her defence if things turned nasty and she was touched by his championship, even though she knew she didn't need it.

She turned back to the staff with a warm feeling in her heart as she switched to the next slide in her presentation. Daniel's support gave her extra confidence and her voice cut through the crowd easily.

'If you look at the screen you'll see the other side of the postcard. It contains a written apology from the company. If you don't feel comfortable talking to the protestors, that's fine. We can understand that, but I would ask for volunteers to hand out the postcards.'

A murmur ran around the room as people read the text Kayleigh had written. It contained an apology, and a promise to take redemptive action to make up for the loss of the trees.

A worker with a cynical face shouted, 'They're just fancy words to shut up them people outside. I can't believe the bosses are going to plant loads more trees.'

Now Peter stepped forward. 'I give you my word that's exactly what we're going to do.'

197

The cynical man didn't look convinced, but many people nodded.

'Fair enough,' said one. 'But what's this about a competition?'

Kayleigh smiled as she explained. 'We're going to plant lots of trees by way of compensation for the felling that took place recently, but that's a short-term plan. The board has decided that Bond's Cycles should support an environmental cause, and the best way to select a good cause or charity is to ask our customers what they think. You'll see that we're asking people to email in with their ideas. The best suggestions will win a mountain bike, and details of the winners and the charity chosen will be posted on our website.'

'Our website's not up to much,' one of the office staff muttered. 'It's only a bit of a catalogue.'

'All that will change, starting tomorrow,' Kayleigh promised, and she couldn't help a naughty grin at Peter. 'The board are now fully aware of how powerful a marketing tool a well-managed website can be.'

Peter smiled ruefully, and turned to his staff to reinforce her message.

'The marketing manager is interviewing web consultants this morning. We want to get moving at once.'

'Makes a change,' one wag shouted.

Kayleigh made no effort to stop the resultant laughter. She wanted the staff feeling good.

When Peter's secretary appeared in a doorway at the end of the room, Daniel slipped over, spoke with her briefly and came back to Kayleigh with a smile lifting his face.

'I didn't think it was possible in such a short time, but the delivery of promotional items is here. Whatever did you promise your friend? His staff must have worked through the night!'

'I called in a few favours,' Kayleigh admitted. 'Can you ask someone to bring them in, please? Do you know if the umbrellas arrived?'

'A thousand of them, all present and correct.'

She couldn't stop a grin from spreading over her face.

'Everything's going to be just fine now!' she said joyously. 'Getting the umbrella printed with the company logo in time was the one thing I was worried about.'

Daniel looked at her in wonder. 'You're only apprehensive about the umbrellas? You have no doubts that one board of directors, two hundred worried workers and five hundred angry protestors will do exactly what you want?'

'Of course they will!' she replied, privately thinking that she would never admit exactly how troubled her sleep had been the night before, or that butterflies in her stomach were reminding her that the protestors hadn't actually gone yet! Instead she smiled airily. 'Piece of cake.'

'You are amazing!' he said.

Two men banged open the canteen doors and pushed in a goods trolley loaded high with brown boxes.

'The caterer's van's arrived an' all,' one said.

'Fantastic! Now we can get moving!'

Kayleigh faced the room again and called out loud, 'If anyone feels they're not up to representing the company, then you're free to stay here, but I do hope all of you will come out and campaign. We need your help, and the more of you who join the team, the faster we can get over this problem and back to work.

'Before you make up your minds, I would like you to know that a large order of fresh coffee and a selection of pastries and doughnuts has just arrived. There is a catering van outside waiting to serve you and the protestors, and guess what? We've even thought of umbrellas.' She picked up a big green umbrella and twirled it around so that everyone could see the bike company logo written large.

'Come on!' she cried. 'Free coffee and doughnuts, an umbrella to take home, and all you have to do is hand out a few postcards.'

For one horrible second she thought people were going to refuse, but then everyone moved towards her and she was nearly trampled in the stampede.

'Are you all right?' Daniel asked, reaching her through the crush.

'Of course! I just need to make sure they take postcards as well as the free brollies!'

She turned to the crowd around her. 'Here, take a handful of these. You need some, too, and so do you. Make sure you take enough to hand around. There are enough umbrellas for the protestors. Take plenty.'

Kayleigh took a handful of postcards herself and followed the surge of workers outside, Daniel staying close to her and holding an umbrella over her head. A light rain still fell, but the air was fresh and the sun showed signs of breaking through. It would be fine soon.

'What sort of coffee do you want?' Daniel asked.

'I'll get some later.'

'You'll get some now, and you'll eat a pastry as well – doctor's orders!' he commanded. 'You've lost weight while you've been away.'

'So have you!' she replied.

He looked at her with such love that her heart lifted as she met his gaze. Despite the fact that he was engaged to Fiona she had the sudden certainty that they belonged together.

'I think my appetite is coming back!' she told him.

He smiled widely in return, and his eyes sparkled. 'What an extraordinary coincidence, so is mine!'

He gestured at the pastry he was holding out to her on a paper plate. 'Please, enjoy your breakfast.'

The cinnamon pastry was scrumptious and the coffee was fresh, hot and delicious.

'This is a good idea,' she admitted, and as Daniel smiled at her her knees went weak.

She couldn't look away from him. His eyes were very bright and very blue, and she knew that she loved him. But they had a job to do.

She turned to the protestors. 'Would anyone like a free drink?'

Standing next to her Daniel called, 'Free coffee! Free pastries! And does anyone need an umbrella?'

'Is that you, Kayleigh?' cried a woman with pink hair and black clothes. 'I didn't recognise you in a suit! Whose side are you on today?'

'The planet's side!' Kayleigh told her, as more people recognised her and came crowding around. 'Always and for ever the planet's side. The guys at Bond's aren't so bad. They made a mistake, but they've learned from it and they're acting to put it right. And they do make bicycles, after all. That's pretty green!'

Kayleigh's heart beat faster as she waited for the woman's pronouncement. Would her fellow eco-warriors turn against her? Some of them could be very, very militant.

'You say Bond's are sorry?' the woman queried, shaking her pink hair.

'Truly sorry,' Kayleigh said, handing her a postcard.

A few seconds later the woman grinned and took a cup of coffee and a pastry.

'I know you'll keep them to it!' she said.

Relief lifted Kayleigh's heart as she greeted more people she knew. Once they understood the new line the bicycle factory was taking, they were happy to shelter under a free umbrella and enjoy a drink and a snack before leaving.

A white television van bristling with antenna and a satellite dish turned through the gates and parked neatly, and a young man in jeans and an army coat got out and came over to her.

'Is it true that Bond's are handing out coffee to the protestors?'

'Sure is,' Kayleigh said, laughing. 'Have some yourself.'

An older man got out of the van and surveyed the scene, frowning.

'Well, it's not news any more, but it might make a positive item to end the programme with,' he said gloomily. 'I need someone from the cycle company for an interview.'

Peter pushed Kayleigh forward. 'Here's the mastermind!'

He stood behind the camera with Daniel and proudly watched Kayleigh give her interview. She was aware of them watching her and she couldn't help smiling back as she explained how sorry Bond's were about felling the trees and invited the viewers to visit the website to nominate an environmental cause for the company to sponsor.

'Well done!' Peter said in his deep voice when she finished. 'You're an absolute genius at public relations. I do hope they broadcast it.'

The rain stopped and the sun came out. The television crew packed up and drove away.

'There's still coffee left! And pastries. Is anybody hungry or thirsty?' Kayleigh called out, but she was speaking to a practically deserted street. There were only about ten protestors left, and all of them were carrying umbrellas boasting the company logo. Her plan had worked.

Peter was ecstatic. 'My dear, I don't know how to thank you! You have succeeded beyond my expectations.'

Kayleigh's glow of satisfaction was short-lived as Fiona came marching towards them, bundled up in a red mackintosh.

'Hello, Daniel darling. Sorry I couldn't get here sooner, but I had a wedding dress fitting this morning. Good heavens – where has everybody gone?'

Daniel smiled proudly at Kayleigh. 'Thanks to Kayleigh the protestors are content that justice will be done and have moved on.'

Peter smiled at Fiona, and then gestured towards a tall blond lad standing by the catering van. 'Mole Man has arrived, by the way – the chap with the blond curls over there who looks like a surfer. I managed to contact him to let him know that the injunction had been lifted and he was welcome here. Do you want to come and have a word with him?'

'Certainly not! He looks like a complete down and out!' Fiona said.

Peter laughed. 'I must admit I was surprised to learn that he's the Duke of Hamble's eldest, Tom. He'll own half of the county one day.'

Fiona's jaw dropped. 'No! Well, perhaps if you're all going to meet him I'll come along...'

Tom turned to greet them, his blue eyes sparkling. 'Yo, Kayleigh!' he cried.

'Hi, Tom,' she replied.

Tom looked warily at Daniel. 'We kind of know each other, right, dude?'

'Kind of,' Daniel agreed, but he was smiling. 'Fiona, do you remember meeting Mole Man before?'

Fiona peered at him, then let out a squeal. 'You're the man with the plastic badgers!

How screamingly funny. Do you still have any?'

Tom smiled at her. 'Nope. I've moved on to the next campaign.'

'Do tell me about it...' Fiona fawned.

One of the factory workers came over to Daniel and Kayleigh to ask, 'What about the woman in the tree?'

Kayleigh looked up at the large oak by the gates. She could see a kind of platform about two thirds of the way up.

'I'll climb up and talk with her.'

Daniel looked at her askance. 'You can't climb a tree in that lovely suit!'

Kayleigh grinned back merrily. 'Watch me!' A ruined suit was a small price to pay if she could persuade the last protestor to go home.

She stood at the bottom of the tree and called up before she attempted to climb it.

'Can we come up and talk with you?'

A head with feathery hair appeared over a branch, a head Kayleigh recognised, and two round black eyes peeped down.

'Kayleigh? Is that you? What are you doing in a suit? You can't climb up here dressed like that.'

Kayleigh laughed. 'I'll manage. Do you want coffee and a pastry, Leila?'

The black eyes sparkled and Leila's head nodded vigorously so that her hair fluttered all around her.

By the time Kayleigh had been to the caterer's van and returned, a ladder had been propped up against the tree. She looked at Daniel.

'You arranged that, I suppose? Well, thank you.'

'I don't know if it'll help. Surely you can't manage it in a pencil skirt and high heels?'

'I'll manage, but I will let you carry the coffee,' she told him.

With both hands free, she didn't find scaling the ladder too difficult and was soon stepping on to the platform her friend had built. It nestled delightfully among the branches and seemed to shelter them from the world.

'This is nice!' Daniel said, scrambling up behind her. 'Look at that glorious view.'

They could see right over the factory buildings to the misty green hills of the Pennines in the distance. Sunlight glinted through the branches and turned the drops of rain that still hung on the leaves into diamonds.

'I love trees,' said Leila, regarding her oak tree fondly. She had a sweetly piping voice and was pretty in an elfin way.

'Have a fresh coffee, Leila. This is Daniel, by the way. I guess you missed all that happened this morning?'

'The birds were up before me today,' Leila admitted, taking a Danish pastry. 'I slept in.'

'Read this, then, and then I'll give you the details,' Kayleigh said, handing over one of the specially printed postcards.

As she explained that the cycle company were promising to put things right, the cosy little platform rocked slightly in the breeze and a shower of drops fell from the branches. The oak leaves fluttered around them like curtains.

'Cool!' Leila said when Kayleigh had finished. 'I'm glad the problem's solved. I hate being away from my forest and now I can go home.'

She put a few things into an orange holdall and slipped down the ladder, leaving Kayleigh and Daniel alone on the platform.

Leaves rustled around them. It was like being alone in the enchanted forest.

'Kayleigh,' Daniel murmured softly.

She met his gaze. There was a world of magic in his look and she felt herself smiling. However crazy their situation might be, she loved him for ever.

'You idiot!' she told him tenderly.

He bowed his head, and it was an effort not to reach out and stroke it.

'I know.' He sighed. 'I'm sorry. I need to apologise. More than apologise – I need to grovel. Can you ever forgive the ignorant, arrogant idiot I was?' He looked at her with such a pleading expression in his eyes that she felt shy and breathless.

Before she could answer he continued: 'You've been away for months and it's nearly two weeks since you got back. That's longer than the time we spent together in the first place. That's a lot of time for a man to think – a lot of time to see where I went wrong.'

Kayleigh had her own confession to make. 'I've had a lot of time to think, too. I should have explained myself better instead of running away.'

'No,' he said, 'it was my fault. I fell in love with your beautiful face and then wanted to change you to fit it. I had no idea what a warm, loving and passionate person you are.'

'If I'd had more confidence in myself, perhaps you would have found it easier to believe in me.'

He shook his head. 'I was ignorant. I'm glad you went away. I'm glad you refused to marry the bonehead I used to be. You're still the most beautiful woman I've ever seen, but now I love all of you, not just your lovely face.'

Happiness lifted her heart as if it was on wings. She couldn't speak, but she reached out her hands towards him, and felt wonderfully secure and loved as he took them and folded them inside his strong warm fingers.

'I'm glad I went to New York,' she confided. 'It's given me a new perspective and a new confidence. I should thank you for making it happen.'

She could see the happiness in his eyes.

'It's very sweet of you to forgive me so completely, but no more than I expected now that I know you. You have a generous heart, Kayleigh.'

They would have kissed, they *wanted* to kiss. Their bodies swayed towards one another – but their lips could not touch. Not yet.

'I love you with all my heart but I'm not free to kiss you,' he said huskily. 'But I'll speak to Fiona today. I have to break it off with her.'

'Poor Fiona…'

He looked at her with sadness in his loving eyes. 'She knows I don't love her. I never did. But somehow she convinced me that I could at least make her and my mother happy. I agreed because it didn't matter to me who I married if it couldn't be you. If you didn't love me…'

'Oh, Daniel, of course I love you.'

His eyes shone as brightly as the sunshine gleaming on the wet leaves around them. 'And I love you. I love you, I trust you, I admire you, and I'll be on your side for ever, no matter what.'

This time there was no warning voice in her heart telling her that, much as she loved him, their marriage would never work. This time her whole being blazed with love in answer to that which radiated from him, and she was secure in the knowledge that she had everything she could possibly want in the world. She had found the missing half of her soul.

'Daniel, I love you, too. I always loved you.'

'I'm so glad you came home,' he murmured.

'I should never have run away.'

He examined her face in that way that he

had, then he lightly kissed her forehead and drew back, sighing deeply and letting go of her hands.

'It's hard not to be able to kiss you properly, but I must speak to Fiona first.'

They exchanged a glance of pure happiness, and then the wind shook the tree branches and a shower of drops sprinkled them both and clung in their hair.

'Let's go down to ground level,' Daniel said. 'Here, let me help you.'

As soon as they reached the car park, Daniel marched across to where Fiona was talking animatedly with Tom. Peter stood nearby, watching. Everyone else had vanished.

Fiona turned a pink and smiling face towards Daniel. 'Hello!' she said briefly, and turned back to Tom.

Daniel cleared his throat. 'Fiona, I have to speak to you, at once and in private.'

'Of course, darling. How about after lunch? I promised Tom that I would make him some carrot soup from a recipe of my grandmother's. She was a very keen vegetarian.'

Fiona smiled at Tom, who gave her an enormous grin. 'Wicked! Do you put herbs in it?'

'Oh, yes, and I roast the carrots as well.

Nanny insisted it improved the flavour.'

Peter smiled at his son and whispered, 'Who would ever have thought Fiona would get on so well with our eco-warrior?'

Daniel gave a wry grin and was about to answer when a gleaming black 4 x 4 with smoked glass windows rumbled through the gates and pulled up, gravel flying from its oversized tyres. Both front doors slammed open, Hugo jumping out of the driver's side and Frederick the passenger side. Both were wearing black clothes, big heavy boots and dark sunglasses, and looked faintly ridiculous, like comic book baddies.

Hugo's jaw dropped in amazement as he took in the deserted factory gates, and Peter smiled at him. 'As you can see, Kayleigh's plan worked tremendously well.'

Hugo scowled so hard that his little brown eyes nearly vanished. He didn't look as if the news pleased him, and soon they learned why as the tailgate of his black vehicle opened and six large security guards emerged. Kayleigh saw Daniel smother a smile, but he was too kind to make any negative comments about Hugo's arrangements.

Frederick glared at Hugo in disgust. 'Wasting our time,' he said.

Hugo didn't seem to know what to say

next, and then Fiona, who was still chatting to Tom and seemed not to have noticed her brother's arrival, laughed at something her companion had said. The sound caught Hugo's attention.

'Fiona!' he shouted.

She turned to him with a pink and smiling face, her usually muddy eyes a lovely sherry colour in the sunshine. 'Hi, Hugo,' she trilled, and then turned back to Tom and carried on chatting.

Hugo strode furiously towards her. 'Why didn't you leave me your key this morning?'

Fiona turned back to him and the colour and the happiness drained out of her face as she recognised the mood her brother was in.

'What do you mean?'

'I mean that I told you to get out! I want all your stuff out of my house by five o'clock today or I'll burn it.'

'But the house is half mine!'

'I don't care. I warned you about voting against me. Get out or you'll be sorry.'

Looking every inch the thug that he was, Hugo strode back to his black off-road vehicle, climbed in like a clumsy bear and slammed the door. The other security men hastily jumped in the back seats as Hugo revved the engine, then the tyres squealed and gravel sprayed as he drove away.

'Heavy dude,' Tom offered into the silence that followed.

Tears were running down Fiona's face. 'He means it. I'll have to move. Daniel...?'

'Of course you must have my house.' Daniel glanced at Kayleigh. 'I'll move in with my parents, if they'll have me.'

Peter grinned broadly. 'It'll be our pleasure.'

Fiona wiped away her tears with a shaking hand. 'I don't know what to do.'

'I'll take you to my place,' Daniel said, but then his mobile phone rang and he rolled his eyes to the sky.

'Yes? I see. Yes. And there's no one else who can operate? I'm in the middle of a crisis... You've tried to contact Dr Walker? I see... There's no help for it then. I'll be with you as soon as I can.'

He looked at Fiona. 'I'm sorry–'

Her face screwed up like a disappointed little girl's. 'Daniel, you can't go! I need you!'

Kayleigh stepped forward. 'He has to go. But I'll help you.'

'And so will I,' Peter promised.

However, Tom waved them both away. He put an arm around the sobbing Fiona and to everyone's astonishment she turned her head into his shoulder and let him hug her.

Tom grinned over the top of her head. 'I'm the main man when it comes to a rescue!' he announced.

Daniel looked at the weeping Fiona with a worried crease between his brows, but then he checked his watch and groaned.

'Every second counts. I must leave.' His eyes met Kayleigh's in appeal and apology.

'I'll make sure she's OK,' she promised.

'Thanks. Here are my house keys. Look after them for her.' He pulled Kayleigh close for a fleeting precious second. 'Remember I love you,' he whispered in her ear, before sprinting to his car and driving away.

Tom grinned at Kayleigh and Peter. 'Chill, guys. The girl will do good with me.'

'Fiona?' Peter questioned.

She lifted her head from Tom's shoulder and wiped her tears. 'I'll be fine, if Tom will help me to move.'

'I'll look after you, girl,' he said, giving her a brotherly thump on her upper arm.

'We'll have to hire a van,' she warned him. 'Hugo will destroy anything I leave behind. He always used to smash my toys when he was angry with me.'

Tom gestured towards a lilac-coloured

Volkswagen camper van covered in brightly-painted flowers and rainbows.

'You're welcome to use my wheels!'

As he watched Fiona drive away in the lilac camper van with Tom, Peter looked around at the deserted car park and gave a huge sigh that came from the bottom of his boots.

'The protest is over, and it's all thanks to you, Kayleigh. I never realised how much I loved the business until I came close to losing it. After four generations of Warner-Bonds, imagine if I had been the one to ruin the family firm?'

He turned to her and smiled at her with those eyes that were so like Daniel's and tenderly kissed her once on each cheek. 'I'm in your debt for ever, my dear – thank you so much.'

Kayleigh smiled back. 'There's still work to be done.'

He smiled. 'Ah, yes – learning the intricacies of website design! Lead the way.'

Chapter Twelve

'She's Disappeared!'

Daniel rang Kayleigh a couple of hours later. He sounded tense and frustrated. 'I need your advice,' he said.

She swung back in her chair and chuckled. 'That doesn't sound like you.'

There was a pause and then he laughed too. 'Cheeky! I'm thinking about Fiona. Hugo was so cruel to her. I don't know if today's the right day to end our engagement. Yet it seems wrong to keep her in the dark.'

Kayleigh thought rapidly. 'Have you spoken to her at all yet?'

'No. I wanted to talk to you first.'

'It is too late to go to your American conference?'

'Not really. I'm not actually scheduled to speak in Boston until Monday. Then I'm supposed to fly across to Florida to give my paper again there. I would like to go. I want to give my paper. There are a few fire-crackers in it that I'm looking forward to unleashing on the medical profession.'

'Then go.'

'I wish you were free to come with me. I want to be with you. This situation is driving me insane.'

'Go to America,' she repeated. 'It'll give us all a few days to regroup.'

He rang off, only to ring back a few minutes later.

'Fiona's not home. I've left a message on her answering machine saying that I need to speak with her when I get back. I'll ring her again when I get to the States.'

Kayleigh tried not to feel sorry for him. After all, this awkward situation was entirely of his own making! Instead she threw herself into her work at the cycle factory.

Thanks to a fresh new design company run by people so young they made Kayleigh feel ancient, an amazing new website was online in only three days. Probably because of the controversy and the spot on TV, within 24 hours of its launch, nearly half a million people had visited the site, most of them also entering the competition to find a worthwhile cause for Bond's sponsor.

Peter and the board were delighted, and at the next meeting Peter approached Kayleigh officially.

'We never in our wildest dreams imagined such a brilliant response. Would you consider working for us permanently?'

'I'm very flattered by your offer,' she hedged, 'and I like the company and everyone here, but...'

Peter smiled in understanding. 'But it's not big enough for a woman of your exceptional talents. You need the challenge of a wider range.'

'I'm thinking of going it alone. In fact, I've almost decided,' she confessed. 'Rushton's Bakery has approached me for a quote and some ideas. It would be a fantastic contract if I got it.'

'You will,' Peter said with certainty. 'I know Shelly Rushton, or Gilday as she is now. I shall recommend you highly to her.'

'Thank you.'

Ruth was smiling. 'You'll never be short of work. There's so much competition for public attention. My church is in desperate need of funds – the roof is simply riddled with beetles, and the estimates to have it put right are terrifying – but none of us has the least idea how to go about fundraising.'

'Would you like me to help?' Kayleigh offered at once.

Ruth shook her head sadly. 'We could

never afford a professional of your calibre.'

'I'm always happy to contribute to charity work, though.'

'Really? Have you worked for a church before?'

Kayleigh shook her head. 'No. So you might prefer to look for someone more experienced than me.'

'Goodness, that's not what I meant at all. We'd love to have you, if you're sure you would like to help us.' She dived into her handbag and pulled out her mobile phone. 'I could ring the vicar now.'

Reverend Tamworth turned out to be the vicar that she had met at the badger-tunnel fund-raising fair all those months ago.

'Small world,' he said, laughing. 'Shall I come into Manchester to meet with you?'

'I could come out to you on Saturday afternoon,' Kayleigh suggested.

Ruth was delighted. 'It's very good of you to give up your free time.'

'I'll have better ideas if I visit the church first,' Kayleigh said, knowing that wasn't the whole story. Her real motive was to fill in the hours before she was free to be with Daniel.

He phoned from America that evening.

'Did they like your paper any better in

Florida than they did in Boston?' Kayleigh asked him.

'Not really! It's amazing how conservative the medical profession can be. But I don't care about my paper, I care only about you. I rang Fiona again last night, but she's still not answering the phone.'

'Perhaps she's on a business trip?'

'She doesn't work. I can't think where she might be,' he fretted.

'Back with Hugo? They might have made up.'

A long sigh crossed the transatlantic connection. 'I've tried to contact her there. I've tried her mother. I've tried her riding stables. I've tried everywhere I can think of, but nobody has seen her. But I'll track her down the moment I get back, and then, Miss Hartley, I shall be free to declare my wild and passionate love to you.'

Kayleigh felt a delicious thrill run down her spine. 'We'll be together in a few days,' she sighed.

'Together forever,' he promised. 'I'll be home on Saturday afternoon. Given the original circumstances and my increasingly urgent messages, I suspect Fiona already knows what it is I want to say to her, but I can't predict how long it'll be before I'm free to see you.'

'I'll wait,' Kayleigh promised. 'My favourite restaurant on the Street of a Thousand Curries is open all night. We could meet there any time.'

'The street of what? Where? I've lived near Manchester all my life and I've never heard of such a place.'

'You must know where I mean – that area with all the Indian restaurants.'

He gave a sudden delighted laugh. 'Well, yes, but I call it Rusholme High Street! Oh, Kayleigh, I'm missing you horribly. What are you doing on Saturday?'

'Going to church,' she told him. 'No, not for a wedding. In fact, I have to wait until all the weddings are finished before I can go. No, I won't tell you why, not until we're together.'

Saturday came and was a glorious day with a definite snap of autumn in it. Despite the distance to Nanton, Kayleigh decided to cycle and enjoy the blue sky and the turning colours of the leaves. Her spirits rose as she turned on to the road that led to the village and whizzed past the village green and the black and white 'magpie' houses. Soon, soon, soon, Daniel would be all hers.

The vicar was waiting for her in front of the church.

'It's so different from the timbered houses,' Kayleigh said, surveying the stone building.

'It's very much earlier. It was built before the Normans arrived.' Reverend Tamworth gazed at his lovely church with a sad look in his eyes. 'So much history and heritage,' he mused.

'We'll save it, just as we saved the badgers,' Kayleigh assured him.

He smiled. 'You haven't seen inside yet. Come in and I'll enjoy showing you. As well as the angels who hold up the ceiling, we have some wonderful fourteenth-century misericords and a carved green man.'

But as he reached for the big brass latch of the wooden door, brisk footsteps rapped up the path, and a large, frumpy lady in a baggy black coat charged towards them with a determined expression on her face.

'George! George! I need a word with you about the decorations for my daughter's wedding,' she announced in a stentorian voice.

Kayleigh thought she heard a sharp intake of breath next to her, but the face he turned to his parishioner was mild and kindly.

'I'm afraid you'll have to excuse us, Ursula. This young lady has come specially from Manchester to help us with the fundraising and I couldn't possibly waste her time.'

The lady snorted and gave Kayleigh a mean look from muddy brown eyes that were about as friendly as a grizzly bear's.

'This is truly important, George. The young lady will excuse us for a few moments, I'm sure.'

Kayleigh murmured something polite and slipped inside the building, thinking 'Ursula' might want a private conversation, but the vicar simply followed her, the woman hot on his heels.

The church was small, and she had a very loud voice. 'My silly daughter tells me she didn't like to ask you to have the walls of the church repainted for the wedding. Well, I said to her, what utter nonsense. As if dear George would mind. Besides, who could like wishy-washy magnolia? A really lovely pale blue would be much more suitable.'

'But, Ursula, we have no plans to repaint the church at present.'

'But it's looking so shabby! You must! Look at this stain here, and that spot on the wall. The new colour might as well be blue.

Here, take this shade chart – the correct colour is marked.'

Rather than take the proffered chart, George Tamworth put his hands in his pockets. 'I don't remember blue being discussed at the parish meeting.'

The woman rolled her brown eyes and waved the shade chart in his face. 'It's well known that men are colour blind. I don't suppose vicars are any different.'

'Why blue?' he asked.

'The bridesmaids will be in ice-blue satin, and I shall be wearing navy.'

A small, worried pucker creased his brow. 'I'm poor at colours, I admit, but I do remember Fiona talking to me about an autumnal theme.'

Kayleigh's attention suddenly sharpened and she regarded the battleaxe with new interest. No, it couldn't be! Could it? Yet the resemblance was there…

'Fiona talks rubbish a good deal of the time,' her loving mother told the vicar. 'But she'll do as she's told.'

'But surely – it's your daughter's big day – she'll have something to say about it.' He had the air of a man grasping at straws.

'My husband always believed in obedient children,' announced Ursula Morton. 'My two were no stranger to strict discipline when they were young and we have never had a moment's trouble with them.'

Kayleigh had never expected to feel sympathy for Hugo and Fiona, but suddenly she wanted to hug the little children they had been. Their childhood sounded miserable.

George Tamworth's kind blue eyes sharpened but now was not the time for what he wanted to say.

'Ursula,' he began carefully, 'I will offer you a compromise on this question of colour. At your own expense, you may arrange to have the church painted any shade you wish, on the condition that immediately after the wedding you have it restored to its original colour, not magnolia but an English heritage shade recommended by the National Trust. Good day to you.'

Ursula stood blinking after him, looking as if she was wondering whether to charge after him or not, but after a few moments she shrugged and went away.

George joined Kayleigh at the front of the church.

'I'm still wondering what a misericord is,' she told him.

The vicar's cheeks were quite crimson; his

encounter with Ursula Morton had clearly ruffled him. But he answered her with ready good manners.

'A misericord is the carved back of a choir seat. Ours have rather lovely carvings of the seasons on them. But perhaps the environment is more your thing than church architecture?'

'It's all part of our world as far as I'm concerned. I'm sure I'll learn a lot as the campaign gets underway.'

His blue eyes looked sad behind his glasses and he took her arm to show her a chart on the wall detailing how much money the church needed to raise, and the congregation's progress towards their target. The total at the top was very high. The amount reached was pitifully low.

'I have an army of willing volunteers,' he told her, 'but the sum we need to raise is simply unobtainable by our normal fund-raising activities. Helena Jones is the choir leader and she does our accounts. She's brilliant at figures, but her conclusions are rather depressing. We'll have to hold three and a quarter million cake raffles in order to save the roof.'

'Is it hard to keep interest going for such a big project?'

'Some of my parishioners do become impatient with the slow pace of raising money from our jumble sales and raffles, but I should tell you now that although some of our members are pressing to introduce scratch cards, I'm very much against anything that could be construed as gambling.'

Kayleigh nodded and smiled. She liked him for his scruples.

'I'll bear that in mind as I construct the campaign.'

He smiled back at her. 'I'd be glad if you would. People might judge all Christians by their contact with our church.'

'Talking about contact, I couldn't find anything about your church on the Internet,' she pointed out.

'Why should there be?'

'You must have a website. Once we start fundraising, people must have a way to get in touch and support your campaign.'

'We have put our address on our leaflets,' he protested mildly.

'That's good, but I'd like you to think bigger. Your church is so beautiful that people from all around the world might want to help save the building. But we have to tell them about it first. Would anybody volunteer to construct a website, do you think?'

Reverend Tamworth looked rueful. 'I doubt if anyone would know how. But I will ask when I make the announcements at the service tomorrow.'

The big church doors crashed wide at that moment and a flock of young people burst in, twittering like swallows. They were followed by a very thin, stooped woman.

'Helena!' called the vicar. 'Do come and meet Kayleigh Hartley.'

Helena had a beautiful smile and eyes so dark they were nearly black.

'Hello, Kayleigh. I look forward to working with you, but excuse me for now. I can't leave these little monkeys for long.'

'These little monkeys' were evidently the choir, and Kayleigh sat in the front pew with the vicar and watched Helena hand out books and marshal them into their places. It was a pleasure to watch their fresh faces and sparkling eyes, but it was the first few bars of their first song that really made Kayleigh sit up straight.

'What wonderful singing! You must do a CD! If we start straight away we could do one for the Christmas market.'

'A CD? Really? Wouldn't it be frightfully

difficult technically?' the vicar asked, looking worried. Kayleigh was beginning to realise that technology wasn't his thing.

'I know a good recording studio. They'll help you through the whole process.'

'And how would we sell it?'

'On your website,' Kayleigh told him firmly.

As soon as the song was over she went to Helena and explained her plan.

'Oh no!' Helena cried, with something very close to panic in her black eyes. 'We aren't good enough.'

'Oh, yes, you are!' Kayleigh insisted. From the quality of the singing she knew Helena must be a wonderful choir leader. All she needed was confidence.

Kayleigh turned to the rows of children. They all stared back at her with bright curiosity.

'What do you think, kids? Shall we record a CD and make lots of money for the church?'

'Yes!' they all roared.

Helena still had a worried pucker between her brows. 'But I wouldn't know where to begin.'

'I'll help you,' Kayleigh promised. 'Take it one step at a time. Could you pick out some favourite Christmas songs and start rehearsing them?'

Helena nodded. 'I could do that.'

'Fantastic!' Kayleigh replied. 'Let's make a start!'

She stayed much longer than she had intended and the sky was a deep navy blue with a fine crescent moon in it as she left the church. A single star hung under the moon and seemed to watch over her. Friendly yellow light shone from the cottage windows all around the green, and Kayleigh paused for a moment to soak up the peace and beauty of the scene. She was proud to play a part, no matter how tiny, in preserving such a delightful part of England's heritage.

Just as she was making sure her bicycle lights were working, her mobile phone rang. It was Daniel.

'Are you home?' she cried eagerly. 'Have you told her?'

There was a long pause before he replied. 'I got back several hours ago, but I haven't been able to tell Fiona anything. She's disappeared.'

Kayleigh felt a clutch of fear at her heart. Such dreadful things could happen.

'You mean, the police are looking for her?'

'No. Apparently she sent a text to her

mother saying that she wanted to think and was going away for a few days. Her phone's been switched off ever since.'

'I see...'

Daniel gave a laugh that was half a sigh. 'I had the strangest conversation with Ursula Morton. In the absence of Fiona she wants me to become involved in painting a church blue or some such ludicrous scheme. She's an extraordinarily tricky woman. It took me some time to convince her that I won't do any such thing.'

Kayleigh decided not to mention for the moment that she had actually met the 'tricky woman'.

'Where does she think Fiona might be?'

'She has no idea.'

'So I suppose we'll have to wait until she turns up,' she said wistfully.

'I have no intention of waiting,' Daniel replied crisply. 'I need to be with you, and nothing's going to stop me. One of my fellow doctors, Sam Gilday, has recommended a private detective agency. They'll find her.'

'A private detective? Isn't that rather extreme?'

'No. I refuse to sit around waiting. I'll never let anything stand between us again. I only became entangled in this ridiculous situation because I was stupid and didn't make every effort to be with you. I should have followed you to America and *made* you come home with me.

'Well, I'll not make the same mistake twice. I'm meeting one of the detectives at Hugo's house to see what leads he can give us, and I've offered them a bonus if they find Fiona within twenty-four hours or less.'

'*One* of the detectives? How many are on the case?'

'The agency employs thirty-four and twenty-six of them are trying to win that bonus!'

Kayleigh's heart glowed inside her. 'I hope they earn it.'

'So do I. I don't want to speak to you on the phone any more – I want to be *with* you. But to be serious, we're also concerned for Fiona's safety. I imagine she's fine, but all the same...'

Kayleigh was bitterly disappointed when none of the detectives claimed that bonus. Hugo had no information as to where his sister might be, but he did say, rather scornfully and disapprovingly, that she often used to run away and hide when she was a small child, so her disappearance didn't surprise him at all.

Daniel was called back by the hospital on Monday for an emergency, and as soon as they had got him there, his secretary set about persuading him not to cancel his operating list.

'It's emotional blackmail,' he grumbled to Kayleigh.

'It makes sense,' she soothed. 'It must be upsetting when someone gets all keyed up for an operation and then it's cancelled.'

Daniel laughed. 'You and my secretary seem to think the same way. I might as well stop arguing now! I can't withstand you both. At least it'll help me to pass the time until we can be together.'

Chapter Thirteen

At Last...

The hours seemed to crawl by over the next two days, and not even finding that she'd won the contract for Rushton's Bakery could lift Kayleigh's heart. She knew Daniel would be working as skilfully as ever, for he had a wonderful ability to shut out the world and concentrate, but she was not so focused.

She started to sketch some ideas, but there was no zest in her and she pushed the drafts away from her.

'I'll have to think of something better!' she muttered. The bakery would be expecting a fresh and dynamic campaign, but her ideas just wouldn't come. She was glad when the telephone rang to distract her, and even gladder when she heard Daniel's voice.

'The agency say they've found Fiona!' he said, but he sounded so worried that Kayleigh's heart swooped into her mouth.

'Is she all right?'

'Physically, yes, but if it *is* Fiona and not a case of mistaken identity, I can't be sure about her mental condition. She's not behaving like the woman I've known all my life.'

'What do you mean? Where is she?'

'I can hardly believe this is true, but according to the detective who found her, she's living in a lilac-coloured camper van in a lay-by on a new bypass near Shrewsbury.'

Kayleigh listened for a stunned moment, and then she started to laugh, a deep, rich, happy laugh that came up from the very soles of her shoes and burst out into the universe.

'What's so funny?' Daniel demanded. 'I'm sure they're wrong. It can't be Fiona.'

'It is,' Kayleigh gasped, still laughing and incredulous. 'If it's a lilac-coloured camper van, it's Fiona all right. Didn't you see Tom's van when you were at the factory? I didn't think anyone could have missed that purple camper van covered in flowers!'

'Mole Man?' Daniel said, and he sounded astounded.

'She let him hug her, do you remember?'

Daniel started to laugh, and there was a carefree sound in his voice that had been missing for a long, long time.

'If it's true, this is a better result than I could have ever imagined, but I need to see it with my own eyes before I'll believe it. I can't imagine Fiona teaming up with an eco-warrior.'

'I can,' Kayleigh said slowly, remembering how happy Fiona had been while she was talking with Tom. 'What will you do now?'

'Drive down to see her, and I want you to come with me. Can you get away?'

Her heart started to sizzle at the idea of being with him. 'I wouldn't miss this for anything!'

She raced up to her bedroom to get changed. Remembering what Daniel had said about the camper van being parked in a lay-by, she dug out her boots and warm clothes, then knocked at her little sister's door.

'Charlene, may I borrow your sleeveless down jacket?'

Charlene was on the floor in black exercise clothes. She turned a cheerful face to her sister. 'Sure. Where are you going?'

'Somewhere cold and outdoors. That's all I know at this point. I'll tell you when I get back. Hey, look at you – you're so flexible!'

Charlene grinned. 'Daniel showed me some great exercises. My leg's as good as new. Hey, that sounds like his car – did you two make up? Where are you going?'

'Tell you later,' Kayleigh cried, and raced down the stairs to the front door.

Daniel was standing on the pavement waiting for her in the cool air, smiling and looking so handsome that Kayleigh longed to throw herself into his arms, but at the last second she hesitated, and so did he. Their eyes met in wordless communication. Better, far better, to wait until he was free.

He spoke for them both when he said, 'Not long now.'

It took several hours to drive to Shrewsbury. The sky was a deep smoke grey and wind turned the leaves on the trees upside down, showing their autumn colours and tossing them around in the air. The roads were busy with commercial traffic and Daniel concentrated on his driving while Kayleigh sat quietly, happy to be with him.

'It should be along this new road somewhere,' Daniel said, flashing her a quick smile before returning his attention to the road. 'I don't know how difficult it'll be to find her.'

'Not difficult at all!' Kayleigh said, pointing at a blue road sign that announced parking in one mile. Tied to it was a large notice lettered with dripping black paint.

'What did that poster say? I was concentrating on the traffic,' Daniel said.

'Something about blackbirds – I couldn't read it properly.'

Daniel shook his dark head. 'There must be a mistake. This can't be Fiona.'

'We'll soon find out,' she said, as the lay-by came into sight. Behind it was a large cemetery. Trees and vegetation veiled the marble tombs and overhung the wall by the parking space.

The lilac camper-van was easy to spot, parked at a jaunty angle next to a large bus with flapping curtains at the windows. Next to the bus, smoke was spiralling upwards from an opening at the top of a kind of tepee. Daniel parked his car carefully and surveyed the scene in front of him.

'It's a mistake,' he said again as they got out into the cold air. The traffic sounded very loud as it rumbled down the busy road and the rain drove down relentlessly. 'This is the last place on earth I would expect to find Fiona.'

But the first person who came to meet them was indeed Fiona; a smiling, happy Fiona dressed in a swirling brown skirt and a waistcoat embroidered with autumn leaves. She waved vigorously when she saw them.

Daniel seemed at a loss for words and Kayleigh couldn't help smiling.

'Hi, Fiona, how are you?'

'Absolutely brilliant!'

'I've never seen you look so well,' Kayleigh said truthfully.

Despite the wet weather, Fiona was glowing. Her face looked softer, and her eyes shone a lovely tawny colour.

'I've never been so happy, and it's all thanks to Tom. Ah, here he is now. Tom, look who's here!'

Tom strolled over to them with the easy grace that always made Kayleigh think of surfing, and put an arm around Fiona. Rain ran down his brown face and his white teeth gleamed as he smiled.

'Cool. How's it going, dudes?'

Daniel looked at the smiling couple and his expression was so grim that for one horrible moment Kayleigh wondered if he was jealous. Then he threw back his head and laughed out loud.

'What do I know about women?' he demanded. 'I was completely wrong about Kayleigh, and now I find I was completely wrong about you, too, Fiona.'

Tom shook wet blond curls out of his eyes.

'That's women for you. Do you like herbal tea?'

The lilac van was tiny inside but spotlessly clean and even cosy, though it was so close to the road that the table vibrated and the teacups rattled whenever the heavy lorries went by. Daniel gestured out of the window at the crumbling cemetery.

'Why here? Why not somewhere more cheerful?'

'We've got a job to do,' Fiona told him, leaning forward earnestly. 'The council are planning to cut down all the trees in the cemetery but rooks have nested there for centuries.'

Kayleigh couldn't help enjoying Daniel's bemused expression as he observed the evangelical fire in Fiona's eyes.

Tom's blue eyes darkened. 'Nobody except us cares about the birds.'

Fiona nodded. 'The council says the trees have to go because the roots are damaging the gravestones. We tried leafleting, and we tried to get the newspaper to write a story about us and get a campaign going, but nobody seems interested. We tried putting plastic rooks on people's lawns, but nobody noticed them. Not even Tom's website worked.'

'There're protests by the gazillion these days. We need a totally cool campaign to get people into the cause, you know.'

Fiona looked at Kayleigh with an oddly pleading, almost humble expression in her brown eyes.

'Kayleigh, can you think of anything? You're so good at this.'

Kayleigh took a sip of her fragrantly steaming herbal tea and flashed them a grin. Her creative juices were flowing again.

'We'll have to think about repairing the damage if we want to get the council on our side. Some kind of employment scheme, perhaps? We could train young people in stonework.'

Tom sat upright. 'You know Stewart? That retired teacher from Lymm?' he said to Kayleigh. 'He was saying that there's funding from the EU for teaching traditional crafts.'

'He's brilliant at schemes like that. Get on to him. And as for raising interest in the birds, let me think. Birds are a bit small to attract attention. But we could all dress up as scarecrows and have a protest march. There'll be no work for scarecrows if all the birds leave.'

Tom laughed and pounded his knee with his hands. 'I love it! That's a wicked idea.'

Daniel laughed, his eyes full of admiration. 'That should get people talking. It's an unusual scheme, but I can see it working. Do you think I would make a good scarecrow?'

She looked into his loving eyes. 'You? You'll dress up as a scarecrow and join our protest?'

His smile was a promise. 'I'm looking forward to it.'

'Your staff will tease you,' she warned.

'Let them!'

'Your boss will think you're associating with odd people.'

'I wouldn't be so sure of that. Did you know that I've persuaded Professor Winston to take up cycling? Maybe I'll ask him to join us.'

Kayleigh's heart melted. 'Daniel, that's amazing.'

'You opened my eyes so that I realise now what a difference one person can make. I think your ideas for saving this beautiful old cemetery sound wonderful.'

'I'll start organising straight away,' Fiona cried, jumping up.

Daniel called her back. 'Before you go, Fiona, may we officially call off our engagement?'

She looked at him with an astonished face. 'Well, of course. I thought we already had! Is that why you came? Daniel, you big old-fashioned silly.'

Tom looked at Fiona with a remarkably soft expression in his eyes. 'Give the dude his ring back.'

Fiona shook her head. 'It's not his ring, it was my grandmother's.' Then she looked at Kayleigh. 'Getting engaged was completely my idea, you know. I bullied him into it! I convinced him that it would make our families happy if we got married, even though he told me he was only agreeing because he thought you weren't coming back.'

Kayleigh hugged Fiona hard. 'Thank you for telling me.'

Daniel stood up to leave and grinned ruefully. 'You'd better tell your mother it's off before she paints Nanton church blue.'

Fiona's happy expression dimmed, but Tom put a reassuring arm around her. 'Hey, I'll be with you,' he reminded her.

She looked at him with such love and trust that a lump sprang into Kayleigh's throat.

She took Daniel's hand as they went out into the rain, skirted the tepee and walked back towards his car.

'It looks like Fiona will be happy. I'm glad.'

'And now we're free to concentrate on our own happiness,' he murmured, and the intensity in his eyes sent her heart into a ridiculous panic.

He started the engine and drove off in a determined fashion.

'Isn't Manchester the other way?' she asked after a minute or two.

'Who says I'm taking you to Manchester?'

'So where…?' she questioned softly.

'I'm taking you somewhere we can be completely alone and undisturbed. Take my phone out of my pocket and put a new voicemail message on it for me. Then turn it off.'

'What shall I say?'

'That Dr Warner-Bond is unavailable until further notice. Put a similar message on your own phone and turn that off as well,' he ordered.

He turned off the busy road into a country lane, and at once the atmosphere was fresher and the sound of the main road soon faded. Kayleigh watched the silver rain slanting over green hedges tipped with autumnal gold and felt happiness welling up within her. He turned left once more, between two thick beech hedges and then over a cattle grid, and rolled to a halt.

'Oh, how lovely!' she exclaimed.

Before them stretched a narrow tarmac strip about a quarter of a mile long, planted with magnificent lime trees. Parkland stretched away on either side of the trees, and at the very end of the avenue nestled a delightful manor house hotel. Leaded windows and pointed chimneys peeped through the flame-coloured leaves of a Boston ivy.

'It looked attractive on the Internet, but the reality is even better,' he observed in satisfaction.

They drove down to the gravel sweep of car park on the left of the house, and had to walk through an arch of clipped yew trees to reach the front door. The garden was autumn bare but a fountain splashed and the flowerbeds were neatly dug. Kayleigh felt as if they were in a fairy tale as they mounted the stone steps that led to the magnificent wooden door of the hotel.

'Dr Warner-Bond?' the receptionist greeted them with a warm smile. 'Please come this way. Lunch will be served in about an hour.

Would you care for coffee in the lounge? We have decaffeinated cappuccino, as you requested.'

The hotel lounge was quintessentially English country house with oil paintings in gilt frames, period wallpaper and comfortable armchairs. An open fire crackled in a friendly way and gave off welcome warmth.

Coffee and biscuits were with them in minutes, but Daniel didn't seem interested in the refreshments. He unzipped his fleece jacket and threw it on to a squashy leather sofa, then took two quick steps and cupped Kayleigh's face with his hands.

'At last!' he said, and kissed her with a passionate hunger.

She sighed as she leaned into him, rejoicing in the solid strength of him. His hands slipped through her hair and then ran down her back.

She turned her head so she could kiss his warm neck, and his lips were soft yet exciting on her temples.

'I can hardly believe we're finally free to be together.'

'Oh, Daniel. I was such an idiot.'

He looked down at her and his eyes blazed with happiness.

'No more running away to America?'

'No more getting engaged to the wrong person?' she riposted indignantly, and he smiled.

'Touché!' He drew her to him. 'I love you,' he said simply. 'Kayleigh, would you do me the very great honour of becoming my wife?'

'You know I will.'

He reached into the pocket of his trousers and drew out a small navy box with a gold Chinese character on the lid, which he flipped open to reveal the diamond engagement ring made by Jade Snow Yao all those months ago.

'Even when I thought I had lost you for ever, I couldn't bear to part with this ring.'

As he slipped the gold band back on her finger, she felt like she was coming home all over again, and as she gazed at the ring, the diamonds floated as much because of the tears in her eyes as the glorious design.

'I'm so happy you kept it safe.'

He captured her left hand to touch the diamond with his lips.

'We can choose a new ring if you'd prefer a fresh start.'

She met his gaze and was tenderly amused by the worry she saw there.

'Never! I'll keep this one with all its memories.'

Joy illuminated his face.

'Do you remember sitting in that beautiful courtyard together?' He cupped her face in his hands again and said urgently, with a mixture of love and solemnity, 'My life would have been a disaster if it wasn't for you. I was so certain that I was right, so stuck in my groove. I owe you everything, Kayleigh. I love you so much. When can we be married?'

There was only one answer to such a question asked in such a way.

'As soon as possible – but not in a blue church!'

The publishers hope that this book has given you enjoyable reading. Large Print Books are especially designed to be as easy to see and hold as possible. If you wish a complete list of our books please ask at your local library or write directly to:

Dales Large Print Books
Magna House, Long Preston,
Skipton, North Yorkshire.
BD23 4ND

This Large Print Book, for people
who cannot read normal print,
is published under the auspices of

THE ULVERSCROFT FOUNDATION